PENGUIN CLASSICS
Night at the Crossroads

'I love reading Simenon. He makes me
— William Faulkner

'A truly wonderful writer . . . marvellously readable – lucid, simple, absolutely in tune with the world he creates'
— Muriel Spark

'Few writers have ever conveyed with such a sure touch, the bleakness of human life'   — A. N. Wilson

'One of the greatest writers of the twentieth century . . . Simenon was unequalled at making us look inside, though the ability was masked by his brilliance at absorbing us obsessively in his stories'   — *Guardian*

'A novelist who entered his fictional world as if he were part of it'   — Peter Ackroyd

'The greatest of all, the most genuine novelist we have had in literature'   — André Gide

'Superb . . . The most addictive of writers . . . A unique teller of tales'   — *Observer*

'The mysteries of the human personality are revealed in all their disconcerting complexity'   — Anita Brookner

'A writer who, more than any other crime novelist, combined a high literary reputation with popular appeal'
— P. D. James

'A supreme writer . . . Unforgettable vividness' — *Independent*

'Compelling, remorseless, brilliant'   — John Gray

'Extraordinary masterpieces of the twentieth century'
— John Banville

GEORGES SIMENON

Night at the Crossroads

Translated by LINDA COVERDALE

PENGUIN BOOKS

PENGUIN CLASSICS

Published by the Penguin Group
Penguin Books Ltd, 80 Strand, London WC2R ORL, England
Penguin Group (USA) Inc., 375 Hudson Street, New York, New York 10014, USA
Penguin Group (Canada), 90 Eglinton Avenue East, Suite 700, Toronto, Ontario, Canada M4P 2Y3
(a division of Pearson Penguin Canada Inc.)
Penguin Ireland, 25 St Stephen's Green, Dublin 2, Ireland (a division of Penguin Books Ltd)
Penguin Group (Australia), 707 Collins Street, Melbourne, Victoria 3008, Australia
(a division of Pearson Australia Group Pty Ltd)
Penguin Books India Pvt Ltd, 11 Community Centre, Panchsheel Park, New Delhi – 110 017, India
Penguin Group (NZ), 67 Apollo Drive, Rosedale, Auckland 0632, New Zealand
(a division of Pearson New Zealand Ltd)
Penguin Books (South Africa) (Pty) Ltd, Block D, Rosebank Office Park, 181 Jan Smuts Avenue,
Parktown North, Gauteng 2193, South Africa

Penguin Books Ltd, Registered Offices: 80 Strand, London WC2R ORL, England

www.penguin.com

First published in French as *La nuit du carrefour* by Fayard 1931
This translation first published 2014
001

Copyright 1931 by Georges Simenon Limited
Translation © Linda Coverdale, 2014
GEORGES SIMENON ® Simenon.tm
MAIGRET ® Georges Simenon Limited
All rights reserved

The moral rights of the author and translator have been asserted

Set in 12.5/15pt Dante MT Std
Typeset by Palimpsest Book Production Ltd, Falkirk, Stirlingshire
Printed in Great Britain by Clays Ltd, St Ives plc

ISBN: 978-0-141-39348-3

www.greenpenguin.co.uk

MIX
Paper from
responsible sources
FSC
www.fsc.org   FSC™ C018179

Penguin Books is committed to a sustainable
future for our business, our readers and our planet.
This book is made from Forest Stewardship
Council™ certified paper.

1. The Black Monocle

Detective Chief Inspector Maigret was sitting with his elbows on the desk, and when he pushed his chair back with a tired sigh, the interrogation of Carl Andersen had been going on for exactly seventeen hours.

Through the bare windows he had observed at first the throng of salesgirls and office workers storming the little restaurants of Place Saint-Michel at noon, then the afternoon lull, the mad six o'clock rush to the Métro and train stations, the relaxed pace of the aperitif hour . . .

The Seine was now shrouded in mist. One last tug had gone past with red and green lights, towing three barges. Last bus. Last Métro. At the cinema they'd taken in the film-poster sandwich boards and were closing the metal gates.

And the stove in Maigret's office seemed to growl all the louder. On the table, empty beer bottles and the remains of some sandwiches.

A fire must have broken out somewhere: they heard the racket of fire engines speeding by. And there was a raid, too. The Black Maria emerged from the Préfecture at around two o'clock, returning later to drop off its catch at the central lock-up.

The interrogation was still going on. Every hour – or every two hours, depending on how tired he was – Maigret would push a button. Sergeant Lucas would awaken from his nap in a nearby office and arrive to take over, glancing briefly at his boss's notes. Maigret would then go and stretch out on a cot to recharge his batteries for a fresh attack.

The Préfecture was deserted. A few comings and goings at the Vice Squad. Towards four in the morning, an inspector hauled in a drug pusher and immediately began grilling him.

The Seine wreathed itself in a pale fog that turned white with the breaking day, lighting up the empty quays. Footsteps pattered in the corridors. Telephones rang. Voices called. Doors slammed. Charwomen's brooms swished by.

And Maigret, setting his overheated pipe on the table, rose and looked the prisoner up and down with an ill humour not unmixed with admiration. Seventeen hours of relentless questioning! Before tackling him, they had taken away his shoelaces, detachable collar, tie and everything in his pockets. For the first four hours they had left him standing in the centre of the office and bombarded him with questions.

'Thirsty?'

Maigret was on his fourth beer, and the prisoner had managed a faint smile. He had drunk avidly.

'Hungry?'

They'd asked him to sit down – and stand up again. He'd gone seven hours without anything to eat and then they had harassed him while he devoured a sandwich.

The two of them took turns questioning him. Between

sessions, they could each doze, stretch, escape the grip of this monotonous interrogation.

Yet they were the ones giving up! Maigret shrugged, rummaged in a drawer for a cold pipe and wiped his damp brow.

Perhaps what impressed him the most was not the man's physical and psychological resistance, but his disturbing elegance, the air of distinction he'd maintained throughout the interrogation.

A gentleman who has been searched, stripped of his tie and obliged to spend an hour completely naked with a hundred malefactors in the Criminal Records Office, where he is photographed, weighed, measured, jostled and cruelly mocked by other detainees, will rarely retain the self-confidence that informs his personality in private life.

And when he has endured a few hours of questioning, it's a miracle if there's anything left to distinguish him from any old tramp.

Carl Andersen had not changed. Despite his wrinkled suit, he still possessed an elegance the Police Judiciaire rarely have occasion to appreciate, an aristocratic grace with that hint of reserve and discretion, that touch of arrogance so characteristic of diplomatic circles.

He was taller than Maigret, broad-shouldered but slender, lithe and slim-hipped. His long face was pale, his lips rather colourless.

He wore a black monocle in his left eye.

Ordered to remove the monocle, he had obeyed with the faintest of smiles, uncovering a glass eye with a disconcerting stare.

'An accident?'

'A flying accident, yes.'

'So you were in the war?'

'I'm Danish. I did not have to fight. But I had a private aeroplane, back home.'

The artificial eye was so disturbing in this young face with pleasant features that Maigret had muttered, 'You can put your monocle back.'

Andersen had not made a single complaint, either about them leaving him standing or their forgetting for so long to give him anything to eat or drink. He could see the street traffic out of the window, the trams and buses crossing the bridge, the reddish sunlight as evening had fallen and now the bustle of a bright April morning.

And he held himself as straight as ever, as if it were only natural, and the sole sign of fatigue was the thin dark shadow underlining his right eye.

'You stand by everything you've said?' Maigret asked.

'I do.'

'You realize how improbable this all sounds?'

'Yes, but I cannot lie.'

'You're expecting to be released, for lack of conclusive evidence?'

'I'm not expecting anything.'

A trace of an accent, more noticeable now that he was tired.

'Do you wish me to read you the official record of your interrogation before I have you sign it?'

He gestured vaguely, like a gentleman declining a cup of tea.

'I will summarize the main points. You arrived in France three years ago, accompanied by your sister, Else. You spent a month in Paris. Then you rented a country house on the main road from Paris to Étampes, three kilometres from Arpajon, at the place called Three Widows Crossroads.'

Carl Andersen nodded slightly in agreement.

'For the last three years, you have lived there in isolation so complete that the local people have seen your sister only a few times. No contact with your neighbours. You bought an old 5CV that you use to do your own shopping at the market in Arpajon. Every month, in this same car, you come to Paris.'

'To deliver my work to the firm of Dumas and Son, Rue du Quatre-Septembre, that's correct.'

'You work designing patterns for upholstery fabrics. You are paid five hundred francs for each pattern. You produce on average four patterns a month, earning two thousand francs . . .'

Another nod.

'You have no male friends. Your sister has no female friends. On Saturday evening, you both went to bed as usual at around ten o'clock. And, as usual, you also locked your sister in her bedroom, which is near yours. You claim this is because she is nervous and easily frightened . . . We'll let that pass for the moment! At seven o'clock on Sunday morning, Monsieur Émile Michonnet, an insurance agent who lives in a house almost a hundred metres from your place, enters his garage to find that his car, a new six-cylinder model of a well-known make, has vanished and been replaced by your rattletrap . . .'

Showing no reaction, Andersen reached automatically for the empty pocket in which he must ordinarily have kept his cigarettes.

'Monsieur Michonnet, who has talked of nothing but his new car ever since he bought it, believes he is the victim of an unpleasant prank. He goes to your house, finds the gate closed and rings the bell in vain. Half an hour later he describes his predicament to the local police, who go to your house, where they find neither you nor your sister. They do, however, discover Monsieur Michonnet's car in your garage and in the front seat, draped over the steering wheel, a dead man, shot point-blank in the chest. His identity papers have not been stolen. His name is Isaac Goldberg, a diamond merchant from Antwerp.'

Still talking, Maigret put more fuel in the stove.

'The police promptly question the employees of the station at Arpajon, who saw you and your sister take the first train for Paris . . . You are both picked up when you arrive at Gare d'Orsay . . . You deny everything . . .'

'I deny having killed anyone at all.'

'You also deny knowing Isaac Goldberg . . .'

'I saw him for the first time, dead, at the wheel of a car that does not belong to me, in my garage.'

'And instead of phoning the police, you made a run for it with your sister.'

'I was afraid . . .'

'You have nothing to add?'

'Nothing!'

'And you insist that you never heard anything that Saturday night?'

'I'm a heavy sleeper.'

It was the fiftieth time that he had given precisely the same answers and Maigret, exasperated, rang for Sergeant Lucas, who swiftly appeared.

'I'll be back in a moment!'

The discussion between Maigret and Coméliau, the examining magistrate to whom the matter had been referred, lasted about fifteen minutes. The magistrate had essentially given up in advance.

'You'll see, this will be one of those cases we get only once in ten years, luckily, and which are never completely solved! And it lands in my lap! Nothing about it makes any sense . . . Why this switching of cars? And why didn't Andersen use the one in his garage to flee instead of walking to Arpajon to take the train? What was that diamond merchant doing at Three Widows Crossroads? Believe me, Maigret – this is the beginning of a whole string of headaches, for you as well as me . . . Let him go if you want. Perhaps you're right to feel that if he can withstand seventeen hours of interrogation, we'll get nothing more out of him.'

The inspector's eyes were red-rimmed from lack of sleep.

'Have you seen the sister?'

'No. When they brought me Andersen, the young woman had already been taken back to her house by the local police, who wished to question her at the scene of the incident. She's still there. Under surveillance.'

They shook hands. Maigret returned to his office, where

Lucas was idly watching the prisoner, who stood with his forehead pressed against the windowpane, waiting patiently.

'You're free to go!' announced Maigret from the doorway.

Calmly, Andersen gestured towards his bare neck and unlaced shoes.

'Your personal effects will be returned to you at the clerk's office. You remain, of course, at the disposition of the authorities. At the slightest attempt to flee, I'll have you sent to La Santé Prison.'

'My sister?'

'You will find her at home.'

The Dane must have felt some emotion after all as he left the room, for he removed his monocle to pass his hand over what had once been his left eye.

'Thank you, chief inspector.'

'You're welcome.'

'I give you my word of honour that I'm innocent . . .'

'Don't mention it!'

Andersen bowed, then waited for Lucas to take him along to the clerk's office.

After witnessing this scene with astonished indignation, a man in the waiting room rushed over to Maigret.

'What? So you're letting him go? That's not possible, chief inspector . . .'

It was Monsieur Michonnet, the insurance agent, the owner of the new six-cylinder car. He walked into Maigret's office as if he owned the place and set his hat down on a table.

'I am here, above all, about the matter of my car.'

A small fellow going grey, carefully but unprepossessingly dressed, constantly turning up the ends of his waxed moustache.

He spoke with pursed lips, weighing his words and trying to appear imposing.

He was the plaintiff! He was the one whom the forces of justice had to protect! Was he not in some way a hero? No one was going to intimidate him, oh no! The entire Préfecture was at his personal service.

'I had a long talk last night with Madame Michonnet, whose acquaintance you will soon make, I trust . . . She agrees with me . . . Mind you, her father was a teacher at the Lycée de Montpellier and her mother gave piano lessons . . . I mention this so that . . . In short . . .'

That was his favourite expression, which he pronounced in a manner both cutting and condescending.

'In short, a decision must be made with all possible speed. Like everyone, even the richest among us, including the Comte d'Avrainville, I bought my new car on the instalment plan. I must make eighteen payments. Mind you, I could have paid cash, but there is no point in tying up one's capital. The Comte d'Avrainville, of whom I just spoke, purchased his Hispano-Suiza in the same fashion. In short . . .'

Breathing heavily, Maigret did not move.

'I cannot do without a car, which is absolutely necessary for me in the exercise of my profession. When you consider that my territory covers everywhere within a thirty-kilometre radius of Arpajon . . . Now, Madame

Michonnet agrees with me on this: we wish to have nothing further to do with a vehicle in which a man has been killed. It is up to the authorities to take the necessary steps and to procure a new car for us, the same model as the other one, and I would like it to be of a burgundy colour, which would not affect the price . . . Mind you, my car was already broken in and running smoothly, and I shall be obliged to—'

'Is that all you have to tell me?'

'I beg your pardon!'

That was another expression he often used.

'I beg your pardon, chief inspector! It's understood that I am prepared to draw upon all my accumulated knowledge and experience of this locality to assist you, but regarding the urgent matter of this car . . .'

Maigret brushed his hand over his forehead.

'Well! I will come to see you soon at your house . . .'

'What about the car?'

'Yours will be returned to you when the investigation has been concluded.'

'But I just finished telling you that Madame Michonnet and I . . .'

'Then do give my regards to Madame Michonnet! Good day, monsieur.'

It was over so quickly that the insurance man had no time to protest. He found himself back on the landing holding his hat, which had been shoved into his hands, and the office boy was calling to him.

'This way, please! First staircase on the left . . . Exit's straight ahead . . .'

As for Maigret, he locked his door and set water to boil on the stove for some good strong coffee.

His colleagues thought he was working, but he had to be woken up an hour later when a telegram arrived from Antwerp.

Isaac Goldberg, 45, diamond broker, rather well known in the trade. Medium-sized business. Good bank references. Travelled weekly by train or plane to Amsterdam, London and Paris to solicit orders.

Luxurious house Rue de Campine, Borgerhout. Married. Two children, 8 and 12.

Madame Goldberg informed, has taken Paris train.

At eleven in the morning the telephone rang: it was Lucas.

'Hello! I'm at Three Widows Crossroads. I'm calling you from the garage a little more than a hundred metres from the Andersens' house. The Danish fellow has gone home. The gate's locked again. Nothing much to report . . .'

'The sister?'

'Must be inside, but I haven't seen her.'

'Goldberg's body?'

'At the hospital morgue in Arpajon . . .'

Maigret went home to his apartment in Boulevard Richard-Lenoir.

'You look tired!' was all his wife said in welcome.

'Pack a bag with a suit and a spare pair of shoes.'

'Will you be away long?'

There was a ragout in the oven. The bedroom window was open and the bed unmade, to air out the sheets. Madame Maigret hadn't had time yet to comb out her hair, still set in lumpy little pin curls.

'Goodbye . . .'

He kissed her. As he left, she remarked, 'You're opening the door with your right hand . . .'

That was unlike him; he always opened it with his left hand. And Madame Maigret wasn't shy about being superstitious.

'What is it? A gang?'

'I've no idea.'

'Are you going far?'

'I don't know yet.'

'You'll be careful, won't you?'

But he was already going downstairs and hardly turned around at all to wave to her. Out on the boulevard, he hailed a taxi.

'Gare d'Orsay . . . Wait . . . How much to drive to Arpajon? . . . Three hundred francs, with the return trip? . . . Let's go!'

He almost never did this. But he was exhausted. He could barely fight off the drowsiness stinging his eyelids.

And wasn't he – just perhaps – a little perplexed, even uneasy? Not so much because of that door he'd opened with his right hand, nor because of that bizarre business of Michonnet's stolen car turning up in Andersen's garage with a dead man at the wheel.

It was rather the Danish fellow's personality that was bothering him.

'Seventeen hours of grilling!'

Hardened criminals, crooks who'd traipsed through all the police stations in Europe hadn't stood up to that ordeal.

Maybe that was even why Maigret had let Andersen go.

That didn't prevent him from falling asleep in the back of the taxi after they'd gone through Bourg-la-Reine. The driver woke him up at Arpajon, in front of the old market with its thatched roof.

'What hotel do you want?'

'Take me to Three Widows Crossroads.'

It was uphill along the oil-slicked paving stones of the main road, lined on both sides by billboards advertising Vichy, Deauville, fancy hotels, brands of automotive fuel.

A crossroads. A garage with its five fuel pumps, painted red. To the left, the road to Avrainville, marked with a signpost.

All around, fields as far as the eye could see.

'This is it!' announced the driver.

There were only three houses. First, the garage owner's, a stuccoed affair hastily erected when business was booming. A big sports car with aluminium coachwork was filling up at the pump. Mechanics were working on a butcher's van.

Across the way, a small villa of millstone grit with a narrow garden, surrounded by a six-foot-high fence. A brass plate: *Émile Michonnet, Insurance.*

The last house was a good hundred metres away. The wall around the grounds hid all but the second storey, a slate roof and a few handsome trees. This building was at least a century old. It was a fine country residence of times gone by, with a cottage for the gardener, outbuildings, poultry houses, a stable and a flight of front steps flanked by bronze *torchères*.

A small concrete pond had dried up. A wisp of smoke rose straight into the air from a carved chimney cap.

That was all. Beyond the fields, a belfry . . . farmhouse roofs . . . a plough abandoned at the edge of some tilled land.

And along the smooth road cars streamed by in both directions, passing one another and honking their horns.

Maigret got out of the taxi with his suitcase and paid the driver, who filled up at the garage before heading back to Paris.

2. The Moving Curtains

Emerging from the roadside, where some trees had concealed him, Lucas walked over to Maigret, who set his suitcase down by his feet. Just as they were about to shake hands, they heard an increasingly loud whistling sound – and suddenly a racing car whipped past so close to them that the suitcase went flying three metres away.

There was nothing left to see. The turbo-charged car had swung around a hay cart and vanished over the horizon.

Maigret made a face.

'Do many of those go by?'

'That's the first one . . . And I could have sworn it was aiming at us!'

It was a grey afternoon. A curtain twitched in a window of the Michonnet villa.

'Is there any place to stay around here?'

'At Arpajon or Avrainville . . . Arpajon's three kilometres away; Avrainville is closer but has only a country inn . . .'

'Take my suitcase there and get us some rooms. Anything to report?'

'Not a thing . . . They're watching us from the villa . . . It's Madame Michonnet. I got a look at her a little while ago. A largish brunette who doesn't appear to be too pleasant.'

'Do you know why this place is called Three Widows Crossroads?'

'I asked: it's because of the Andersen house, which dates from the revolution. In the old days it was the only house here. In the end, it seems that fifty years ago three widows lived in it, a mother and two daughters. The mother was ninety years old, a helpless invalid. The elder daughter was sixty-seven, the other at least sixty. Three old fusspots, so stingy they bought nothing locally and lived off their kitchen garden and poultry yard . . . The shutters were never opened. Weeks would go by without a glimpse of them. The elder daughter broke her leg at some point, but people learned about it only after she was dead. Quite a strange story! When a long time had passed without anyone hearing the slightest noise from the Three Widows house, people got to talking . . . The mayor of Avrainville decided to come and see for himself – and he found all three of them dead. They'd been dead for at least ten days! There was a lot of newspaper coverage at the time, apparently. A local schoolteacher, fascinated by this mystery, even wrote a booklet in which he claims that the daughter with the broken leg hated her still-active sister so much that she poisoned her, and the mother wound up poisoned as well . . . The elder sister supposedly starved beside the two corpses because she couldn't get herself anything to eat!'

Maigret stared at what he could see of the house's top storey. Then he considered the Michonnets' new villa, the even newer garage, the cars going by on the main road at eighty kilometres an hour.

'Go and get those rooms, then come back and join me.'

'What are you going to do?'

The inspector shrugged, then walked to the gate of the Three Widows house. It was a good-sized building, surrounded by three or four hectares of grounds graced by a few majestic trees.

A sloping lane ran alongside a lawn and up to the front steps, then on to a garage that had once been a stable, its roof still bearing a pulley.

Nothing stirred. Aside from a thread of smoke, there was no sign of life behind the faded curtains. In the gathering dusk, some farm horses in a distant field were plodding back home.

Maigret noticed a little man taking a walk along the road, his hands stuck deep into the pockets of his flannel trousers, a pipe between his teeth, a cap on his head. The man came right up to him the way neighbours do out in the countryside.

'You're the one in charge of the investigation?'

He was wearing slippers and had no collar on, but his jacket was of fine grey English cloth and he sported an enormous signet ring on one finger.

'I own the garage at the crossroads . . . I saw you from my place . . .'

Definitely a former boxer: he'd had his nose broken. His face looked as battered as an old copper pot. His drawling voice was husky, coarse, but very self-assured.

'What do you make of this business with the cars?'

The man laughed, revealing some gold teeth.

'If there weren't a stiff involved, I'd find the whole thing hilarious. You can't possibly understand – you don't know the guy across the way, Milord Michonnet, as we call him. A stand-offish fellow who wears collars *this* high and patent-leather shoes . . . Then there's Madame Michonnet! You haven't seen her yet? Huh! Those people complain about anything and everything, go running to the police because the cars make too much noise when they stop at my garage pumps . . .'

Maigret didn't encourage or discourage the man. He simply stared at him in a way that disconcerted most talkative people but had no effect on the garage owner.

A baker's van drove by and the man in slippers yelled, 'Hey there, Clément! . . . Your horn's been fixed! Just ask Jojo for it!'

Turning back to Maigret, he offered him a cigarette and carried on.

'Michonnet had been talking about getting a new car for months, was pestering all the car dealers, myself included! He wanted discounts, ran us ragged . . . The coachwork was too dark, too light; he wanted a burgundy colour – not *too* burgundy, but definitely *burgundy* . . . Well, he ended up buying the car from a colleague of mine in Arpajon. You've got to admit, it was a damn fine joke to have the car turn up a few days later in the Three Widows garage! I'd have given anything to see our gentleman's face that morning when he found the old jalopy instead of the six-cylinder job! . . . Pity about the dead man, which spoils everything. Because a corpse is a corpse, after all, and such matters deserve our respect . . . Say! You'll drop by the garage, won't you, and have a drink? No watering holes at the crossroads, but we'll get some yet! If I can just find the right fellow to run a place, I'll back him for it . . .'

The man must have noticed that Maigret wasn't responding to his patter, because he held out his hand.

'See you later, then . . .'

He strolled off at the same pace, stopping to talk to a farmer passing by in a one-horse cart. Over at the Michonnet villa, there was still a face behind the curtains.

In the evening the surrounding countryside had a monotonous, stagnant air about it, and sounds carried a long distance: a horse neighing, a church bell pealing perhaps ten kilometres away . . .

The first car with its headlamps on went by, but they could hardly be seen in the twilight.

Maigret reached for the bell-pull hanging to the right of the gate. Rich, mellow tones rang through the garden, followed by a long silence. At the top of the steps, the front door did not open, but from behind the house came the crunch of gravel. A tall form appeared; a pale face, a black monocle.

Carl Andersen showed no emotion as he approached and he bowed his head slightly when he opened the gate.

'I knew you would come . . . I suppose you want to see the garage. The prosecutor's office has sealed the premises, but you must have the necessary authority . . .'

He was wearing the same clothes as at Quai des Orfèvres, an elegantly cut suit that was beginning to show signs of wear.

'Is your sister here?'

It was already too dark to notice any change in his

expression, but Andersen did feel the need to resettle the monocle in his eye-socket.

'Yes . . .'

'I would like to see her.'

A brief hesitation. Andersen nodded again.

'Please follow me.'

They walked around to the back of the house, where all the ground-floor rooms had tall French windows that opened directly on to a terrace overlooking a fairly large lawn.

There were no lights in any of the upstairs bedrooms. At the far end of the grounds, veils of mist twined around the tree trunks.

'Allow me to show you the way . . .'

Andersen led Maigret from the terrace into a large drawing room all draped in shadow. The cool yet heavy evening air followed them in, bringing with it the smell of wet grass and leaves. A single log shot a few sparks up the chimney.

'I will call my sister.'

Andersen had not lighted any lamps or even appeared to notice that night was falling. Left alone, Maigret walked slowly up and down the room, stopping before an easel on which sat a sketch in gouache. It was a modern design for a fabric pattern, with bold colours and a strange motif.

But not as strange as the way the room conjured up for Maigret the memory of the three widows of long ago . . .

Some of the furniture must have been theirs. There

were Empire armchairs with flaking paint and threadbare silk, and rep curtains that had hung there for fifty years.

Some pine bookshelves had been built along one wall, however, and were piled with paperbound books in French, German, English and no doubt Danish as well.

And the white, yellow or multicoloured covers were in stark contrast to an old-fashioned hassock, some chipped vases and a carpet worn almost through in the centre.

The twilight was darkening. A cow lowed in the distance. From time to time, a faint humming pierced the silence, intensifying until a car whizzed by on the road and the engine's rumbling at length died away.

In the house, nothing! Perhaps just a few creaks or scratching sounds. Perhaps just some tiny undecipherable noises suggesting the possibility of life.

Carl Andersen came in first. His white hands betrayed a certain nervous anxiety. He stood still and mute for a moment by the door.

A faint movement on the stairs.

'My sister Else,' he announced at last.

She stepped forwards, her silhouette slightly blurred in the dim light. She stepped forwards like a film star, or rather, like the perfect woman in an adolescent's dream. Was her dress of black velvet? It was darker than anything else, in any case, and made its deep, magnificent mark on the dusk. And what little light still drifted in the air seemed to settle on her fine blonde hair and matte complexion.

'I hear you wish to speak to me, chief inspector. But first, please do sit down.'

Her accent was stronger than Carl's and her voice melodious, dropping gently at the ends of words.

And her brother stood by her as a slave stands near the sovereign he is sworn to protect.

She advanced a few steps and only when she was quite close did Maigret realize that she was as tall as Carl. Her slim hips emphasized her willowy silhouette. She turned to her brother.

'A cigarette!'

Nervously, clumsily, he hurried to offer one. She picked up a lighter and the flickering red of the flame fought, for an instant, with the dark blue of her eyes.

Afterwards the darkness weighed more heavily, so heavily that the inspector, feeling uneasy, looked around for a light switch and, finding none, murmured, 'May I ask you to light a lamp?'

He had to call on all his self-possession, for this scene was too theatrical for him. Theatrical? Disorienting, rather, like the perfume that had invaded the room with Else's entrance.

Above all, a scene too estranged from normal life. Perhaps just too strange altogether! That accent . . . Carl's perfect manners and his black monocle . . . That mixture of sumptuous luxury and distressing old relics . . . Even Else's dress, which wasn't the sort of dress one sees in the street, at the theatre, or in society . . .

Why was that? It had to be the way she wore it. Because the style – the cut – was simple. The dress clung to her figure, covering even her neck, revealing only her face and hands.

Andersen was leaning over a table, removing the glass chimney from an oil lamp dating back to the three old ladies, with a tall porcelain base decorated with faux bronze. It cast a circle of light two metres wide in its corner of the drawing room. The lampshade was orange.

'Excuse me . . . I hadn't noticed that all the chairs have things piled on them.'

Andersen removed books from the seat of an Empire armchair and set them down in a heap on the carpet. Else was smoking, standing perfectly straight, a statue sheathed in velvet.

'Your brother, mademoiselle, has told me that he heard nothing unusual last Saturday night. He seems to be a very heavy sleeper.'

'Very,' she repeated, exhaling a wisp of smoke.

'You heard nothing either?'

'Nothing particularly unusual, no.'

She spoke slowly, like a foreigner who must translate her thoughts from her native language.

'You know that we are on a main road. The traffic hardly slows down at all at night. Every evening from eight o'clock on, market lorries driving to Les Halles in Paris go past and they make a lot of noise. On Saturdays we also have tourists heading for Sologne and the Loire. Our sleep is interrupted by the sounds of engines and brakes, loud voices . . . If this house were not so cheap . . .'

'Had you ever heard of Isaac Goldberg?'

'Never.'

Outside, it was not yet completely dark. The lawn was

intensely green and each blade of grass stood out so distinctly that it seemed possible to count them all.

Although the grounds had not been kept up, they were still as picturesque as a stage set at the opera. Every clump of bushes, every tree, even every branch was in just the right place. And the background of fields with a farmhouse roof put the finishing touch to this harmonious vision of the French heartland.

On the other hand, in the drawing room with its old furniture were books with foreign titles, words that Maigret didn't understand. And these two foreigners, the brother and sister . . . Especially the sister, who struck a discordant note . . .

A note that was too voluptuous, too lascivious? Yet she herself was not provocative. Her gestures were unaffected, and she held herself in a natural way.

But this simplicity did not suit such a décor. The inspector would have felt more at home with the three old ladies and their monstrous passions!

'Will you allow me to have a look around the house?'

Neither Carl nor Else seemed to mind. She sat down in an armchair, while he picked up the lamp.

'If you'll just follow me . . .'

'I suppose you use the drawing room, for the most part?'

'Yes, that's where I work and where my sister spends most of her day.'

'You have no servant?'

'You already know how much I earn. It isn't enough for me to hire any help.'

'Who prepares the meals?'

'I do.'

He said this easily, without any embarrassment or shame, and as the two men entered a corridor, Andersen pushed open a door and held the lamp just inside the kitchen, murmuring, 'Please excuse the clutter.'

The place was worse than cluttered. It was sordid. A spirit stove encrusted with boiled milk, sauces, grease, on a table covered with a scrap of oilcloth. Tag ends of bread. The remains of an escalope in a frying pan sitting right on the table and dirty dishes in the sink.

Out in the corridor again, Maigret glanced back at the drawing room, where the only light was now the glow from Else's cigarette.

'We don't use the dining room or the morning room at the front of the house. Would you like to see them?'

The lamp shone on some piled-up furniture and a rather nice parquet floor, on which potatoes lay spread out. The shutters were closed.

'Our bedrooms are up there . . .'

The staircase was wide; one step creaked. The smell of perfume grew stronger as they went upstairs.

'Here is my room.'

A simple box mattress set on the floor, as a divan. A rudimentary dressing table. A large Louis XV wardrobe. An ashtray overflowing with cigarette butts.

'You smoke a lot?'

'In the morning, in bed . . . Perhaps thirty cigarettes, while I read.'

In front of the door opposite his, he said quickly, 'My sister's bedroom.'

But he did not open the door, and when Maigret did, Anderson scowled.

He was still holding the lamp and did not bring it into the room. The perfume was now so cloying that the inspector almost gagged.

The entire house lacked style, order, luxury. A campsite furnished with old odds and ends.

But here in the dim light the inspector had the feeling of a warm, cosy oasis. The floor was completely covered with animal skins, including a splendid tiger pelt serving as a bedside rug.

The bed itself was of ebony, covered with black velvet, on which lay some rumpled silk underwear.

Andersen was edging down the hall with the lamp, and Maigret followed him.

'The three other bedrooms are empty.'

'Which means that your sister's is the only one overlooking the road . . .'

Without answering, Carl pointed out a narrow staircase.

'The service staircase. We don't use it. If you'd care to see the garage . . .'

They went downstairs single file in the dancing light of the oil lamp.

In the drawing room, the red dot of a cigarette remained the only illumination. As Andersen advanced, the lamplight invaded the room, revealing Else lounging in an armchair, gazing with indifference at the two men.

'You haven't offered the chief inspector any tea, Carl!'

*what a bizarre
scenario !!* ASW 3
4 NOV., 2014

'Thank you, but I never drink tea.'

'Well, I want some! Would you like a whisky? Or perhaps . . . Carl! Please . . .'

Carl, self-conscious and a little on edge, set down the lamp and lit a small spirit stove on which sat a silver teapot.

'What may I offer you, inspector?'

Maigret could not put his finger on what was bothering him. The atmosphere was intimate and yet haphazard. Up on the easel, large flowers with crimson petals were in full bloom.

'So,' he said, 'first someone stole Monsieur Michonnet's car. Goldberg was murdered in that car, which was then placed in your garage. And your car was driven to the insurance agent's garage.'

'Unbelievable, isn't it!'

Else spoke in a soft, lilting voice as she lit another cigarette.

'My brother insisted that because the dead man was found at our place, we would be accused . . . He tried to run away . . . As for me, I didn't want to. I was sure that people would understand that if we had really killed anyone, it would not have been in our interest to—'

She broke off, looking for Carl, who was rummaging around in a corner.

'Well, aren't you going to offer the inspector anything?'

'Sorry . . . I . . . We don't seem to have any more . . .'

'It's always the same with you! You never think of anything . . . You must excuse us, monsieur . . . ?'

'Maigret.'

'. . . Monsieur Maigret. We drink very little alcohol and—'

There was the sound of footsteps outside, where Maigret now saw that Sergeant Lucas was looking for him.

3. Night at the Crossroads

'What is it, Lucas?'

Maigret was standing at the French windows, with the uneasy atmosphere of the drawing room at his back and, before him, the face of Lucas in the cool shadows of the grounds.

'Nothing, chief . . . I wanted to know where you were . . .'

And a slightly sheepish Lucas tried to see inside the house over the inspector's shoulder.

'You booked me a room?'

'Yes. And there's a telegram for you. Madame Goldberg is arriving tonight by car.'

Maigret turned around: Andersen was waiting with bowed head; Else was smoking and wiggling one foot impatiently.

'I will probably return to question you again tomorrow,' he told them. 'My respects, mademoiselle.'

Else nodded to him with gracious condescension. Carl offered to walk the policemen back to the gate.

'You're not going to look at the garage?'

'Tomorrow . . .'

'Listen, chief inspector . . . This may seem somewhat strange to you . . . I'd like you to make use of me if I can be helpful in any way. I know that I am not only a foreigner, but your prime suspect as well. Yet another reason for me to do my utmost to find the guilty man. Please don't hold my awkwardness against me.'

Maigret looked him right in the eye. He saw the sadness in that eye, which slowly turned away. Carl Andersen relocked the gate and went back to the house.

'What came over you, Lucas?'

'Something was bothering me . . . I got back from Avrainville a while ago. I don't know why, but this cross-roads suddenly gave me such a bad feeling . . .'

The two men were walking in the dark along one side of the road. There weren't many cars.

'I've tried to reconstruct the crime in my mind,' continued Lucas, 'and the more you think about it, the more bewildering it becomes.'

They were now abreast of the Michonnet villa, which formed one point of a triangle, the other two of which were the garage and the Three Widows house, all more or less equidistant from one another. Connecting them all, the smooth, shining ribbon of the road, running like a river between two rows of tall trees.

No light could be seen over at the Three Widows house. Two windows were illuminated at the insurance agent's villa, but dark curtains allowed only a thin streak of light to escape, an uneven line, revealing that someone was peeking through the curtains to look outside.

Over by the garage: the milk-white globes atop the pumps, plus a rectangle of harsh light streaming from a workshop resounding with hammer blows.

The two policemen had stopped, and Lucas, who was one of Maigret's oldest colleagues, explained his reasoning.

'First thing: Goldberg had to have come here. You saw the corpse in the morgue at Étampes? You didn't? A man of forty-five, definitely Jewish-looking. A short, stocky guy with a tough jaw, a stubborn brow, curly hair like sheep's wool . . . Showy suit . . . Nice linen, and monogrammed. Someone used to living well, giving orders, spending freely . . . No mud, no dust on his patent-leather shoes, so even if he came to Arpajon by train, he did not cover the three kilometres to get here on foot! My theory is that he arrived from Paris, or maybe Antwerp, by car.

'The doctor says that his dinner had been completely digested at the time of death, which was instantaneous. And yet a large quantity of champagne and toasted almonds was found in his stomach. No hotel proprietor in Arpajon sold any champagne on Saturday night or early Sunday morning, and I defy you to find a single toasted almond anywhere in that town.'

With a screech of rattling iron, a lorry went by at fifty kilometres an hour.

'Consider the Michonnets' garage, sir. The insurance agent has had a car for only one year. His first one was an old wreck that he simply kept in the padlocked wooden shed that opens on to the road. He hasn't had time to have another garage built, so the new car was stolen from the shed. Someone had to drive it to the Three Widows house, open the gate, then the garage, take out Andersen's old heap and leave Michonnet's car in its place . . . And to top it off, stick Goldberg behind the wheel and shoot him dead point-blank. Nobody saw or heard a thing! . . . *Nobody has an alibi!* . . . I don't know if you've got the same feeling I have about this, but when I was coming back from Avrainville a little while ago, while it was growing dark, I was completely at sea . . . I get the sense that there's something wrong with this case, something weird, almost malignant . . .

'I went up to the gate of the Three Widows house . . . I knew you were in there. The façade was dark, but I could make out a halo of yellow light in the garden.

'It's idiotic, I know! But I was afraid! Afraid for you, understand? . . . Don't turn around too quickly . . . It's Madame Michonnet, lurking behind her curtains . . .

'I must be wrong about this, but I'd swear that half the drivers going by are giving us odd looks . . .'

Maigret glanced from one point to another of the triangle. The fields had vanished, flooded in darkness. To the right of the main road, across from the garage, the road to Avrainville branched off, not planted with trees like the highway but lined on one side by a string of telegraph poles.

Eight hundred metres away, a few lights: the outlying houses of the village.

'Champagne and toasted almonds!' grumbled the inspector.

He began walking slowly, stopping in front of the garage as if out for a stroll. In the glare of an arc lamp, a mechanic in overalls was changing a tyre on a car.

It was more of a repair shop than a garage. About a dozen cars were there, all old models, and one of them, stripped of its wheels and engine, was just a carcass hanging in the chains of a pulley.

'Let's go and have dinner! When is Madame Goldberg due to arrive?'

'I don't know. Sometime this evening.'

The inn at Avrainville was empty. A zinc counter, a few bottles, a big stove, a small billiard table with rock-hard cushions and torn felt, a dog and cat lying side by side . . .

The proprietor was the waiter; his wife could be seen in the kitchen, cooking escalopes.

'What's the name of the garage owner at the crossroads?' asked Maigret, swallowing a sardine served as an appetizer.

'Monsieur Oscar,' replied the inn-keeper.

'How long has he been in this area?'

'Maybe eight years . . . Maybe ten . . . Me, I've a horse and cart, so . . .'

And the man continued serving them half-heartedly. He was not a talker. He even had the shifty look of someone on his guard.

'And Monsieur Michonnet?'

'He's the insurance agent.'

That was it.

'Will you have red or white?'

He spent a long time trying to fish out a piece of cork that had fallen into the bottle and in the end just decanted the wine.

'And the people in the Three Widows house?'

'I've never seen them . . . Not the lady, anyway, since it seems there's one there . . . The highway's not really part of Avrainville.'

'Well done?' called his wife from the kitchen.

Maigret and Lucas fell silent, lost in their own thoughts. At nine o'clock, after a synthetic calvados, they went back out to the road, paced up and down for a while, then finally headed for the crossroads.

'She's not coming . . .'

'I'd like to know what Goldberg was doing out here. Champagne and toasted almonds! . . . Did they find any diamonds in his pockets?'

'No. Just a bit over two thousand francs in his wallet.'

The garage was still lit up. Maigret noticed that Monsieur Oscar's house was not by the side of the road but behind the workshop, which meant its windows could not be seen.

Dressed in overalls, the mechanic sat eating on the running board of a car. And suddenly, just a few steps away from the policemen, the garage owner himself came out of the darkness on the road.

'Good evening, gentlemen!'

'Good evening,' grunted Maigret.

'A lovely night! If this keeps up, we'll have wonderful weather for Easter.'

'Tell me,' the inspector asked bluntly, 'does your place stay open all night?'

'Open, no! But there's always a man there who sleeps on a cot. The door's locked. Regular customers ring the bell when they need something.'

'Do you get much traffic on the road at night?'

'Not a lot, no, but it never stops. Lorries on their way to Les Halles . . . This region's known for its early fruits and vegetables, especially its watercress. The drivers sometimes run out of petrol, or need some little repair made . . . Would you like to join me for a drink?'

'No, thanks.'

'Your loss . . . but I won't insist. So! You haven't sorted out this business with the cars yet? You know, Monsieur Michonnet is going to worry himself sick over it. Especially if he isn't issued another six-cylinder car right away!'

A headlamp gleamed in the distance, growing larger. A rumbling sound. A shadow went past.

'The doctor from Étampes!' murmured the garage owner. 'He went to see a patient in Arpajon. His colleague must have invited him for dinner . . .'

'You know every vehicle that goes past here?'

'Many of them . . . Look! Those two side-lamps: that's watercress for Les Halles. Those fellows can never bring themselves to use their headlamps . . . And they take up the entire road! . . . Evening, Jules!'

A voice replied from up in the cab of the passing lorry, and then the only thing to see was the small red tail-light, which soon dissolved into the night.

Somewhere, a train, a glowing caterpillar that stretched out into chaos of the night.

'The 9.32 express . . . Listen, you're sure you won't have anything? . . . Say, Jojo! When you've finished your supper, check the third pump, it's jammed.'

More headlamps. But the car went on by. It was not Madame Goldberg.

Maigret was smoking constantly. Leaving Monsieur Oscar in front of his garage, he began to walk up and down, trailed by Lucas, who kept talking softly to himself.

Not a single light in the Three Widows house. The policemen went past the gate ten times. Each time Maigret automatically looked up at the window he knew was Else's.

Then came the Michonnet villa, brand new, nondescript, with its varnished oak door and silly little garden.

Then the garage, the mechanic busy repairing the petrol pump, Monsieur Oscar dispensing advice, both hands stuck in his pockets.

A lorry from Étampes on its way to Paris stopped to fill up. Lying asleep atop the heap of vegetables was the relief driver, who made this same journey every night at the same hour.

'Thirty litres!'

'How's it going?'

'Can't complain!'

The clutch growled and the lorry moved off, down the hill to Arpajon at sixty kilometres an hour.

'She won't be coming now,' sighed Lucas. 'Probably decided to spend the night in Paris . . .'

After they'd covered the 200 metres up and down from the crossroads three more times, Maigret veered off abruptly towards Avrainville. When they reached the inn, there was only one lamp still burning and no one in the café.

'I think I hear a car . . .'

They turned around. And two headlamps were indeed

shining in the direction of the village. A car was turning slowly in front of the garage. Someone was talking.

'They're asking for directions.'

The car came towards them at last, illuminating the telegraph poles one after another. Maigret and Lucas were caught in the light, standing across the road from the inn.

The sound of brakes. The driver got out and opened a door to the back seat.

'Is this the right place?' asked a woman's voice from inside.

'Yes, madame. This is Avrainville. And there's the traditional branch of fir over the front door of the inn.'

A leg sheathed in silk. A foot placed on the ground. An impression of fur . . .

Maigret was about to walk towards the woman.

At that moment there was a loud bang, a cry – and the woman fell headlong, literally crashing to the ground, where she lay curled up in a ball while one of her legs kicked out spasmodically.

Maigret and Lucas looked at each other.

'Take care of her, Lucas!' shouted the inspector.

But already a few seconds had been lost. The chauffeur stood stunned, rooted to the spot. A window opened on the second floor of the inn.

The shot had come from the field to the right of the road. As he ran, the inspector drew his revolver from his pocket. He could hear something, footsteps thudding softly on clayey soil . . . But he couldn't see a thing: the car's headlamps were shining so brightly straight ahead that they flooded everywhere else with darkness.

Turning around he yelled, 'The headlamps!'

When nothing happened, he yelled it again. And then there was a disastrous misunderstanding: the driver, or Lucas, turned one of the headlamps towards the inspector.

Now he was spotlit, a huge figure in black against the bare ground of the field.

The murderer had to be farther on, or more to the left – or the right – but in any case, outside that circle of light.

'God almighty, the headlamps!' yelled Maigret one last time.

He was clenching his fists in rage, running in zigzags like a hunted rabbit. That glare was disrupting even all perception of distance, which is why he suddenly saw the garage's pumps less than a hundred metres away.

Then there was a human figure, quite close, and a voice saying hoarsely, 'What's going on?'

Furious and humiliated, Maigret stopped short, looked Monsieur Oscar up and down and saw there was no mud on his slippers.

'Did you see anyone?'

'Just a car asking the way to Avrainville.'

The inspector noticed a red light on the main road heading towards Arpajon.

'What's that?'

'A lorry for Les Halles.'

'He stopped?'

'Long enough to take twenty litres . . .'

They could hear the commotion going on over by the inn and the headlamp was still sweeping the deserted field. Maigret suddenly noticed the Michonnet villa, crossed the road and rang the bell.

A small spy hole opened.

'Who's there?'

'Detective Chief Inspector Maigret. I would like to speak with Monsieur Michonnet.'

A chain and two bolts were undone. A key turned in the lock. Madame Michonnet appeared, anxious, even upset, impulsively darting furtive glances up and down the main road.

'You haven't seen him?' she asked.

'He's not here?' replied Maigret gruffly, with a glimmer of hope.

'I mean . . . I don't know . . . I . . . I just heard a shot, didn't I? . . . But do come in!'

She was about forty, plain, with prominent features.

'Monsieur Michonnet stepped out for a moment to . . .'

On the left, the door to the dining room was open. The table had not been cleared.

'How long has he been gone?'

'I don't know . . . Perhaps half an hour . . .'

Something moved in the kitchen.

'Do you have a servant?'

'No. It might be the cat . . .'

The inspector opened the kitchen door and saw Monsieur Michonnet himself, coming in through the garden door, mopping his face. His shoes were caked with mud.

There was a moment of surprised silence as the two men looked at each other.

'Your weapon!' said the inspector.

'My . . . ?'

'Your weapon, quickly!'

The insurance agent handed him a small revolver he'd pulled from a trouser pocket. All six of its bullets were still there, however, and the barrel was cold.

'Where have you been?'

'Over there . . .'

'What do you mean by "over there"?'

'Don't be afraid, Émile! They wouldn't dare touch you!' exclaimed Madame Michonnet. 'This is too much, really! And when I think that my brother-in-law is a judge in Carcassonne . . .'

'Just a moment, madame: I am speaking to your husband . . . You were at Avrainville just now. What did you go there to do?'

'Avrainville? Me?'

He was shaking, trying in vain to put up a front, but seemed genuinely dumbfounded by his predicament.

'I swear to you, I was over *there*, at the Three Widows house! I wanted to keep an eye on them myself, since—'

'You didn't go into the field? You didn't hear anything?'

'Wasn't there a shot? Has anyone been killed?'

His moustache was drooping. He looked at his wife the way a kid looks at his mother when he's in a tight spot.

'I swear, chief inspector! . . . I swear to you . . .'

He stamped his foot, and two tears rolled down his cheeks.

'This is outrageous!' he cried. 'It's my car that was stolen! It's my car they found the body in! And no one will give my car back to me, when I'm the one who worked fifteen years to pay for it! And now I'm the one accused of—'

'Be quiet, Émile! I'll talk to him!'

But Maigret didn't give her the chance.

'Are there any other weapons in the house?'

'Only this one revolver, which we bought when we had the villa built . . . And the bullets are even the same ones the gunsmith put in himself.'

'You were at the Three Widows house?'

'I was afraid my car would be stolen again . . . I wanted to conduct my own investigation . . . I entered the grounds – or rather, I climbed up on the wall.'

'You saw them?'

'Who? Those two? The Andersens? Of course! . . . They're in the drawing room. They've been quarrelling for an hour now.'

'You left when you heard the shot?'

'Yes. But I wasn't sure it was a gunshot . . . I only thought so . . . I was worried.'

'You saw no one else?'

'No one.'

Maigret went to the door and, opening it, saw Monsieur Oscar coming towards him.

'Your colleague has sent me, chief inspector, to tell you that the woman is dead. My mechanic has gone to inform the police in Arpajon. He'll bring back a doctor . . . And now, will you excuse me? I can't leave the garage unattended.'

At Avrainville, the pale headlamp beams could still be seen, illuminating a section of wall at the inn and some shadowy figures moving around a car.

4. *The Prisoner*

Head down, Maigret was walking slowly in the field, where the growing corn was beginning to dot the earth with pale green.

It was morning. The sun was out and the air was vibrant with the songs of invisible birds. In Avrainville, Lucas was standing outside the inn door, waiting for representatives of the prosecutor's office and keeping an eye on the car Madame Goldberg had hired in Paris on Place de l'Opéra for her journey.

The wife of the diamond merchant from Antwerp was laid out upstairs on an iron bed. A sheet had been thrown over her corpse, which the doctor had partly unclothed the night before.

It was early on a fine April day. In the very field where Maigret, blinded by the headlamps, had chased the murderer in vain and now advanced step by step, following the traces left in the darkness, two farm workers loaded a cart with beets they were harvesting from a hillock while their horses waited quietly.

The double row of trees along the main road sliced through the countryside. The red petrol pumps at the garage sparkled in the sunlight.

Slow, stubborn, quite possibly in a bad mood, Maigret was smoking. The footprints found in the field seemed to prove that Madame Goldberg had been shot dead with a rifle, for the murderer had not come within thirty metres of the inn.

The footprints were unremarkable: smooth soles, average size. The trail curved around to wind up at the Three Widows Crossroads, keeping a more or less equal distance from the Andersens' house, the Michonnet villa and the garage.

In short, this trail proved nothing! It introduced no new lead and Maigret, stepping out on to the road, was biting down on his pipe stem rather grimly.

He saw Monsieur Oscar at his door, his hands in the pockets of his baggy trousers and a smug expression on his common-looking face.

'Up already, chief inspector?' he shouted across the road.

At that same moment someone pulled up between Maigret and the garage: it was Carl Andersen in his little old car.

He was wearing gloves and a fedora and had a cigarette between his lips. He doffed his hat.

'May I have a word with you, chief inspector?'

After rolling down his window, he went on in his usual polite manner.

'I did want to ask your permission to go to Paris, and was hoping to find you here . . . I'll tell you why I must go: today is the 15th of April, the day I am paid for my work for Dumas and Son. It's also the day when the rent is due . . .'

He smiled apologetically.

'Quite ordinary errands, as you see, but urgent ones all the same. I'm low on funds.'

When he removed his monocle for a moment to re-settle it more securely, Maigret turned his head away because he did not like looking into that staring glass eye.

'And your sister?'

'Precisely . . . I was about to bring this up: would it be too much to ask you to have someone look in on the house from time to time?'

Three dark, official-looking cars came up the hill from Arpajon and turned left towards Avrainville.

'What's going on?'

'They're from the public prosecutor's office. Madame Goldberg was killed last night as she was getting out of a car at the inn.'

Maigret watched his reaction. Across the street, Monsieur Oscar was strolling idly up and down in front of his garage.

'Killed!' repeated Carl. Suddenly nervous, he said, 'Listen, chief inspector: I must get to Paris! . . . I can't stay here without any money, especially on the day when I have to pay all my local bills, but as soon as I get back I want to help find the murderer. You will allow me to do this, won't you? I don't know anything for certain, but I feel . . . I don't know how to put this . . . I'm beginning to see some kind of pattern here . . .'

He had to pull in closer to the pavement because a lorry driver coming back from Paris was honking his horn to get by.

'Off you go, then!' exclaimed Maigret.

Carl tipped his hat and took a moment to light another

cigarette before letting in the clutch, whereupon the jalopy went down the hill and puttered up the next one.

People were moving around over by the three cars that were parked just outside Avrainville.

'Sure you wouldn't like a little something?'

Maigret frowned at the smiling garage owner, who just wouldn't stop offering him a drink.

Filling a pipe, he walked off towards the Three Widows house, where the tall trees were alive with the fluttering and chirping of birds. The Michonnet villa was on his way.

The windows were open. Wearing a dust cap, Madame Michonnet was upstairs in the bedroom, shaking out a rug.

Unshaven, his hair uncombed, wearing no collar, her husband was downstairs smoking a meerschaum with a cherry-wood stem and looking out at the road with a glum, abstracted air. When he noticed the inspector, he avoided greeting him by making a show of cleaning out his pipe.

A few minutes later Maigret was ringing the bell at the Andersens' front gate, where he waited in vain for ten minutes. All the shutters were closed. The only sound was the constant twittering of the birds, which transformed every tree into a bustling little world.

In the end Maigret shrugged, examined the lock and let himself in with a passkey. As on the previous day, he walked around the house to the drawing room.

He knocked but, again, without success. Then, grumbling and obstinate, he went inside, where his eye fell upon the open phonograph. There was a record on the turntable.

Why did he start the machine? He would have been at a loss to explain. The needle was scratchy. An Argentinean orchestra played a tango as the inspector started up the stairs.

The door to Carl Andersen's bedroom stood open. Near a wardrobe Maigret saw a pair of shoes that seemed to have recently been cleaned, for the brush and tin of polish sat beside them and the floor was dotted with crumbled, dried mud.

The inspector had made paper tracings of the footprints found in the field. He compared them with the shoes. A perfect match.

And yet he never so much as blinked. He didn't seem the least bit pleased. He went on smoking, as grumpy as he'd been all morning.

'Is that you?' a woman's voice inquired.

Maigret hesitated . . . He could not see who was speaking: the voice had come from Else's room, but the door was closed.

'It's me,' he finally replied, as indistinctly as he could.

Then, a long silence.

'Who's there?' the voice asked abruptly.

It was too late to fool her.

'Detective Chief Inspector Maigret. I was here yesterday. I'd like to speak to you for a moment, mademoiselle.'

More silence. Maigret tried to guess what she could possibly be doing behind that door, beneath which gleamed a thin line of sunlight.

'I'm listening,' she said at last.

'If you'd be good enough to open the door . . . I can certainly wait, if you need time to dress.'

That annoying silence again.

A little laugh, and then, 'What you ask of me is somewhat difficult, chief inspector!'

'Why is that?'

'Because I'm locked in. So you will have to speak without seeing me.'

'Who locked you in?'

'My brother Carl . . . I am the one who asks him to, whenever he goes out, because I'm so terribly afraid of prowlers.'

Without saying anything, Maigret pulled out his passkey and quietly inserted it in the lock. His throat felt tight; was he troubled by any untoward thoughts?

And when the bolt shifted, he decided not to open the door before announcing first, 'I'm going to come in, mademoiselle . . .'

A strange sensation: he was in a dark, drab corridor – and stepped immediately into a setting alive with light.

Although the shutters were closed, the horizontal slats admitted great beams of sunshine.

The entire room was thus a jigsaw puzzle of darkness and light. The walls, objects, even Else's face were as if striped in luminous bands. Then there was the young woman's heavy perfume, plus such incidental details as the silk underwear tossed on to a bergère, the Turkish cigarette smouldering in a china bowl on a lacquered pedestal table, and finally there was Else, lounging on the black velvet couch in a deep red peignoir.

Eyes wide open, she watched Maigret come towards her with amused astonishment and, just perhaps, a tiny tremor of fear.

'What are you doing?'

'I wanted to talk to you. Please forgive me if I'm disturbing you . . .'

She laughed like a little girl. When her peignoir slipped off one shoulder, she pulled it up again but remained lying on or, rather, nestled in the low couch striped with sunlight like the rest of the room.

'You see? . . . I wasn't doing much of anything. I never do!'

'Why didn't you go to Paris with your brother?'

'He doesn't want me to. He says having a woman around gets in the way when men discuss business.'

'You never leave the house?'

'But I do! I take walks around the property.'

'That's all?'

'We have three hectares here, enough for me to stretch my legs, don't you think? . . . But do sit down, chief inspector. It's rather funny, having you here in secret . . .'

'What do you mean?'

'That my brother will have a fit when he gets back. He's worse than any mother. Worse than a jealous lover! He is the one who looks after me and he takes this responsibility seriously, as you can see.'

'I thought you were the one who wanted to be locked in, because of your fear of burglars.'

'There's that, too . . . I've grown so used to solitude that now I am afraid of people.'

Maigret had sat down in a large upholstered armchair and placed his bowler on the rug. And whenever Else looked at him he turned his face away, still unable to meet her gaze with his usual composure.

The previous day, she had simply seemed mysterious to him. In the dim light, a formal, almost regal figure, she'd had the presence of a film star, and their first meeting had taken on a theatrical air.

Now he was trying to discover her human side, but something else was bothering him: the very intimacy of their encounter.

Else relaxing in her peignoir, dangling a slipper from the tip of a bare foot in that perfumed bedchamber, while the middle-aged Maigret sat slightly flushed, his hat on the rug . . .

Wasn't that a perfect illustration for *La Vie Parisienne*?

Rather clumsily, the inspector put his pipe away in his pocket even though he hadn't cleaned it out.

'So, you find it boring here?'

'No . . . Yes . . . I don't know . . . Do you smoke cigarettes?'

She waved towards a pack of Turkish cigarettes, the price of which was marked on the band: 20 francs 65 centimes. Maigret recalled that the Andersens lived on 2,000 francs a month, and that Carl had been obliged to hurry and collect his wages so as to pay the rent and local bills on time.

'Do you smoke a lot?'

'A pack or two a day . . .'

She held out a delicately engraved lighter, then heaved

a sigh that caused the neckline of her peignoir to open a little more revealingly.

The inspector did not immediately hold it against her, though. Among the clientele of luxury hotels he had seen showily dressed foreign women whom the average citizen would have taken for tarts.

'Your brother went out, last night?'

'You think so? . . . I have no idea . . .'

'Didn't you spend the evening arguing with him?'

She showed her perfect teeth in a big smile.

'Who told you that? Did he? We sometimes squabble, but nicely. As a matter of fact, I scolded him yesterday for not receiving you properly. He's so unsociable! And he was already like that as a boy . . .'

'Did you live in Denmark?'

'Yes. In a big castle beside the Baltic . . . A very dreary castle, all white amid dusty green foliage . . . Do you know the country? So gloomy! And yet, it is beautiful . . .'

As her gaze grew distant with nostalgia, she felt a shiver of pleasure.

'We were rich, but our parents were quite strict, like most Protestants. Personally, I pay no attention to religion, but Carl is still a believer . . . Less so than his father, who lost all his fortune through clinging stubbornly to his principles. We left Denmark, Carl and I . . .'

'That was three years ago?'

'Yes . . . Just imagine! My brother was destined to become an important dignitary of the Danish court – and here he is, forced to earn his living designing dreadful fabrics . . . In Paris, in the second- and third-class hotels where we had to stay, he was horribly unhappy. He had the same tutor as our crown prince! But he preferred to bury himself out here.'

'And bury you at the same time.'

'Yes . . . I'm used to it. I was a prisoner in our parents' castle, too. I was kept away from all the girls who might have become my friends, supposedly because they weren't my social equals.'

Her expression changed with striking abruptness.

'Do you think that Carl has become . . . I'm not sure how to put it . . . abnormal?'

And she leaned forwards, as if to hear the inspector's reply as quickly as possible.

'You're afraid of . . . ?' exclaimed Maigret in surprise.

'I didn't say that! I didn't mean anything! Please excuse me . . . You've started me talking . . . I don't know why I trust you like this . . . So . . .'

'Does he behave oddly at times?'

She shrugged wearily, crossed and uncrossed her legs, then stood up, uncovering for an instant a flash of skin between the folds of the peignoir.

'What do you want me to say to you? I don't know any more. Ever since that business with the car . . . Why would he have killed a man he didn't know?'

'You're sure you have never seen Isaac Goldberg?'

'Yes . . . As far as I know . . .'

'You and your brother never went to Antwerp?'

'We stayed there one night, three years ago, when we arrived from Copenhagen . . . No, Carl could not do such a thing! If he has become somewhat strange, I'm sure that his accident is more to blame than our financial ruin. He was handsome! He still is, when he wears his monocle. But otherwise . . . Can you see him kissing a woman without that bit of black glass? That staring eye in its red-rimmed socket . . .'

She shuddered.

'That has to be the main reason my brother hides himself away . . .'

'But he's keeping you hidden along with him!'

'What difference does that make?'

'You're being sacrificed.'

'That's the lot of every woman, especially a sister. It isn't quite the same thing here in France. In our country, as in England, only the eldest male counts in the family, the son who will carry on the name.'

She was growing agitated, puffing hard on her cigarette. She paced up and down through the patterns of sunshine and shadow in the shuttered room.

'No! Carl could not have killed him. That was all a mistake. Wasn't it because you realized this that you let him go? . . . Unless . . .'

'Unless?'

'But you would never admit this! I know that when the police haven't enough proof, they sometimes release a suspect so that they can catch him for good later on . . . That would be despicable!'

She stubbed out her cigarette in the china bowl.

'If only we hadn't chosen this awful crossroads . . . Poor Carl, who wanted to be left alone . . . But we're less on our own here, chief inspector, than in the most crowded neighbourhood in Paris! Across the way are those impossible, ridiculous, narrow-minded people who spy on us, especially her – with that white dust cap every morning and her crooked chignon in the afternoon . . . Then that garage, a little farther on . . . Three groups, three camps is more like it, and all at about the same distance from one another . . .'

'Did you ever have any contact with the Michonnets?'

'No! The man came once, peddling insurance. Carl showed him the door.'

'And the garage owner?'

'He has never set foot here.'

'Was it your brother who wanted to make a run for it on Sunday morning?'

She was quiet for a moment, hanging her head, her cheeks pink.

'No,' she sighed at last, almost inaudibly.

'It was you?'

'Yes, me . . . I hadn't thought things through. The idea that Carl could have committed a crime almost drove me crazy. I'd seen him in such distress the day before . . . So I dragged him along after me . . .'

'Didn't he swear to you he was innocent?'

'Yes.'

'You didn't believe him?'

'Not at first . . .'

'And now?'

She took her time, pronouncing each syllable distinctly.

'I believe that, in spite of all his misfortunes, Carl is incapable of deliberately doing anything evil . . . But listen, chief inspector, he'll probably be getting back home soon and if he finds you here, God knows what he'll think!'

And yet, there was something almost flirtatious, if not provocative, about her smile.

'You will defend him, won't you? You'll get him out of all this? I would be so grateful!'

She held out her hand to him and, as she did so, the peignoir fell slightly open once again.

'Goodbye, chief inspector.'

He picked up his hat and sidled from the room.

'Could you lock the door again, so that he won't notice anything?'

A few moments later, Maigret was going downstairs, crossing the drawing room with its motley collection of furniture, stepping out on to the terrace bathed in sunshine that was already warm.

Cars were humming along the road. The front gate did not creak when he locked it behind him.

As he passed the garage, a mocking voice called out, 'Good for you! You're a brave one, that's for sure!'

It was Monsieur Oscar, in a jovial, man-of-the-people mood.

'Come on!' he added. 'Take the plunge and have a drop with me! Those fellows from the prosecutor's office have already left, so you can easily spare a minute . . .'

The chief inspector hesitated, wincing as a mechanic scraped his file across a piece of steel clamped in a vice.

'Ten litres!' called a motorist waiting by one of the pumps. 'Anyone around, in there?'

Monsieur Michonnet, as yet unshaven and without his

shirt collar, was standing in his tiny garden looking over the fence at the road.

'Finally!' exclaimed Monsieur Oscar when Maigret made a move to join him. 'Plain and simple, that's how I like folks. Not like that snob at the Three Widows!'

5. The Abandoned Car

'This way, inspector! . . . Nothing fancy, eh! This is just a working man's home here . . .'

He pushed open the door of the house behind the garage and they walked directly into a kitchen that must also have served as a dining room, for the breakfast dishes still sat upon the table.

A woman in a pink housecoat of heavy crêpe stopped polishing a copper tap.

'Come over here, honey, and meet Detective Chief Inspector Maigret . . . My wife, inspector! She could afford her own maid, mind you . . . but then there'd be nothing left to do and she'd be bored!'

The woman was neither ugly nor pretty. She was about thirty. Her housecoat was cheap-looking and unflattering, and she stood awkwardly before Maigret, watching her husband.

'Well, go and fetch us an aperitif! . . . An Export Cassis, chief inspector? . . . You'd rather we went into the drawing room? No? That's fine! I never stand on ceremony, myself. Right, honey? . . . No, not those ones – get some highball glasses!'

He leaned back in his chair. He was wearing a pink shirt, no waistcoat, and he slipped his hands inside his belt, cradling his ample belly.

'Exciting, isn't she, the lady over at the Three Widows house . . . Mustn't make a point of it in front of my wife, but between ourselves, she's certainly easy on a man's eyes. Only problem is, she has a brother . . . or so *he* says! A "knight of doleful countenance" that one is – and he spends his time spying on her . . . I've even heard it said around here that when he goes off for an hour, he locks her in – and does the same every night! That sound to you anything like a brother and sister, hmm? . . . Cheers! . . . Say, honey, go and tell Jojo not to forget he's to fix the lorry for that fellow from Lardy.'

Hearing a noise that sounded like a 5CV engine, Maigret turned towards the window.

''Tisn't him, inspector! I can tell you exactly from here, blindfolded, what's passing on the road. That old heap belongs to the power-house engineer. You're waiting for our snob to come back?'

According to an alarm clock on a shelf, it was eleven o'clock. Through an open door Maigret could see a telephone on the wall out in the corridor.

'You haven't touched your drink . . . Well, here's to your investigation! Listen, don't you find something comical in this whole affair? The idea of switching the cars, and especially the bit about pinching the six-cylinder beauty from that stuffed shirt across the way . . . Because that's just what he is – a stuffed shirt! I swear to you, we've got the bottom of the barrel here for neighbours . . . But I've enjoyed watching you coming and going since you arrived yesterday. Particularly when you squint at people as though you suspect the whole lot of them . . . Mind you, I've a cousin on my wife's side who was in the police, too. Gambling Squad. He spent every afternoon at the races, and the best part of the joke? He passed me tips! Well, down the hatch! . . . So, honey, all taken care of?'

'Yes . . .'

For a moment the young woman, who had just come in, stood wondering what she should do next.

'Come on, have a drink with us. The chief inspector isn't snooty, he won't refuse to drink your health because you've got your hair in curlers . . .'

'Would you mind if I make a phone call?' said Maigret abruptly.

'Be my guest! You turn the handle . . . If it's for Paris, they'll connect you right away.'

The inspector looked in the directory for the number of Dumas and Son, the fabric manufacturers to whom Carl Andersen had gone to receive some money.

The phone call was brief. The cash clerk who spoke to Maigret confirmed that Andersen had two thousand francs coming to him that day but had not yet shown up at the premises in Rue du Quatre-Septembre.

When Maigret returned to the kitchen, Monsieur Oscar was rubbing his hands together with great relish.

'You know, I'd rather come right out and say how much fun I'm having. Because I know the score! Something happens at the crossroads . . . there are just three households here . . . it's only natural to suspect us all. Oh yes you do! Don't pretend otherwise. I saw how you were looking at me and how you didn't want to come and have a drink here! . . . Three houses! The insurance agent seems too big a fool to be capable of committing a crime. The snob is an imposing gentleman . . . And that leaves yours truly, a poor working guy who's clawed his way up to being his own man but doesn't know how to talk proper. A former boxer! If you ask after me at police headquarters in Paris, they'll tell you I was picked up a few times in raids, because I used to like dancing the Java in the Rue de Lappe music halls, especially when I was a boxer. Another time I had a go at a cop who was picking on me . . . Bottoms up, chief inspector!'

'No, thanks.'

'You're not going to refuse! A fizzy Export Cassis never hurt anyone . . . You see, I like to put my cards on the table. It bothers me to see you skulking around my garage as if you were watching me on the sly. Right, honey? . . . Didn't I say so last night? "The chief inspector's here! Well, then, let him come in! Let him rummage around everywhere! Let him search me! And then admit that I'm a stand-up guy and innocent as a baby." What really interests me about this whole thing is the cars – because when you get right down to it, the case revolves around cars . . .'

Half past eleven! Maigret stood up.

'Another phone call to make.'

With a worried frown, he asked for police headquarters and told an inspector to send the description of Andersen's little car out to all police stations as well as the border posts.

The four aperitifs Monsieur Oscar had put away had brought a gleam to his eyes and roses to his cheeks.

'Oh, I know you'll refuse to join us for some veal ragout.

Especially seeing as we eat in the kitchen here . . . Ah!
Here's Groslumeau's lorry back from Les Halles: you must
excuse me, chief inspector . . .'

He went outside. Maigret was left alone with the young
woman, who was tending to her ragout with a wooden
spoon.

'Quite a card, your husband!'

'Yes . . . He's a cheerful sort.'

'And gets tough at times, right?'

'He doesn't like being contradicted. But he's a good fellow.'

'Chases a few skirts?'

No reply.

'I bet he goes out on the town now and again.'

'Like all men . . .'

Her voice had turned bitter. They could hear snatches
of conversation over by the garage.

'Put that over there! . . . Good! . . . Yes . . . We'll change
your back tyres tomorrow morning.'

Monsieur Oscar returned in a fine humour, as if he felt
like singing and playing the fool.

'Come on! Sure you won't tuck into some lunch with
us, chief inspector? We could bring up a bottle from the
cellar! . . . Why are you making that face, Germaine? . . .
Women! Moody things, always changing on you.'

'I've got to get back to Avrainville,' announced Maigret.

'Should I drive you back? Wouldn't take a minute . . .'

'No, thank you. I'd rather walk.'

Maigret stepped outside into a bath of warm sunshine,
and on the road to Avrainville a yellow butterfly led
the way.

A hundred metres from the inn he encountered Sergeant Lucas, who had come out to meet him.

'Well?'

'You called it! The doctor extracted the bullet, which did come from a rifle.'

'Nothing else?'

'Yes, there's information from Paris. Isaac Goldberg arrived there in a Minerva sports car he used for travelling and which he drove himself. That's the car he must have driven here from Paris.'

'And that's all?'

'We're still waiting for replies from the Belgian police.'

The driver of the hired car that had delivered Madame Goldberg to her own death had left in his vehicle.

'The body?'

'They took it to Arpajon. The examining magistrate is worried and asked me to tell you to work quickly. His main concern is that the papers in Brussels and Antwerp might splash this affair all over their front pages.'

Humming to himself, the inspector went inside the inn and sat down at his assigned table.

'Do you have a telephone here?'

'Yes! But there is no service between noon and two o'clock, and it's now half past twelve.'

The inspector ate in silence. Seeing that he was pre-occupied, Lucas tried a few times to strike up a conversation, but in vain.

It was one of the first lovely days of spring. After lunch Maigret dragged his chair into the inn courtyard and sat down by a wall, in the company of the ducks and chickens, where he dozed in the sun for half an hour.

At two on the dot, however, he was standing at the telephone, clinging to the receiver.

'Hello! Police Judiciaire? . . . You haven't located that car we're looking for yet? . . .'

The inspector began walking around and around the courtyard. Ten minutes later he was called back to the phone: Quai des Orfèvres was on the line.

'Detective Chief Inspector Maigret? . . . We have just this moment received a call from Jeumont . . . The car has been found there, abandoned across from the train station. We assume that the driver preferred to cross the border on foot or by train.'

Maigret hung up only for an instant, then asked for the offices of Dumas and Son. He was informed that Carl Andersen had still not shown up to collect his two thousand francs.

When Maigret and Lucas walked past the garage at around three o'clock, Monsieur Oscar popped out from behind a car to ask brightly, 'How's it going, chief inspector?'

Maigret merely waved at him and continued on to the Three Widows house.

The doors and windows of the Michonnet Villa were shut but, yet again, the policemen noticed the dining-room curtains twitching.

The garage owner's cheerfulness seemed once more to

have aggravated the ill humour of the inspector, who was puffing furiously on his pipe.

'Now that Andersen has made a run for it—' began Lucas quietly.

'Stay here!'

The inspector entered the grounds and house of the Three Widows property just as he had that morning. In the drawing room he sniffed the air, looked quickly around and noticed wisps of smoke hovering in the corners of the room, which smelled strongly of freshly smoked tobacco.

Without even thinking about it he grasped the butt of the revolver in his pocket before going upstairs, where he could hear phonograph music and recognized the tango he had played that morning.

The music was coming from Else's room. When he knocked, it ceased immediately.

'Who's there?'

'The inspector.'

A short laugh.

'In that case, you know what to do. I can't let you in . . .'

The passkey did its job again. The young woman was wearing the same clinging black dress as the day before.

'Are you the one who has kept my brother from coming home?'

'No. I have not seen him since early this morning.'

'Then they must not have had his payment ready at Dumas. Sometimes he has to go back there in the afternoon . . .'

'Your brother has tried to cross the border into Belgium. As far as I know, he has succeeded.'

She stared at him in astonishment – and some disbelief.

'Carl?'

'Yes.'

'This is some kind of test, isn't it?'

'Can you drive?'

'Drive what?'

'A car.'

'No! My brother has never been willing to teach me.'

Maigret had not taken the pipe from his mouth and was still wearing his hat.

'Have you left this room?'

'Me?'

She laughed. A merry, musical laugh. And more than ever, she was wreathed in what American movies portray as sex appeal.

For a woman can be lovely without being alluring, while other, less classically beautiful women unfailingly inspire desire or sentimental feelings.

Else aroused both: she was at once woman and child, creating her own aura of voluptuous attraction. And yet, whoever looked into her eyes was astonished to find her gaze as limpid as a little girl's.

'I don't understand what you mean . . .'

'Someone has been smoking downstairs in the drawing room within the last half-hour.'

'But who?'

'That's what I'm asking you.'

'And how do you expect me to know that?'

'This morning, that phonograph was downstairs.'

'Impossible! . . . How could that . . . Wait, inspector! I

hope you don't suspect me of anything! You seem different, strange . . . Where is Carl?'

'I'm telling you, he has left the country.'

'That's not true! It can't be! Why would he do that?
Besides, he would never leave me alone here! . . . That's
crazy! What would happen to me, all on my own?'

It was bewildering. Without any warning, without
making grand gestures or even raising her voice, she had
become touching, pitiable. It was in her eyes . . . Dismay
beyond words. An expression of helplessness, of suppli-
cation.

'Tell me the truth, chief inspector! Tell me Carl isn't
guilty! If he were, then it would mean he had gone
mad! I refuse to believe that! . . . It frightens me . . . His
family . . .'

'Do you know of any insanity there?'

She turned her head away.

'Yes, his grandfather died in a fit of madness. And one
of his aunts is in an asylum. But no, not Carl! I know
him . . .'

'Have you eaten any lunch?'

Startled, she looked around her and replied in surprise,
'No!'

'Aren't you hungry? It's three o'clock.'

'I think I am hungry, yes.'

'In that case, go and have lunch. There is no longer any
reason for you to remain locked in. Your brother will not
be coming back.'

'That's not true! He will come back! He would never
leave me all alone.'

'Come on . . .'

Maigret was already out in the corridor, still frowning and still smoking his pipe. He did not take his eyes off the girl, but when she brushed past him it had no effect on him.

Downstairs she seemed even more disoriented.

'It was always Carl who served our meals . . . I don't even know if there's anything to eat.'

A loaf of bread turned up in the kitchen, at least, and a tin of condensed milk.

'No, I can't, I'm too upset. Go away! . . . No, wait – don't leave me! . . . Oh, this horrible house. I have never liked . . . What's that? Out there!'

She pointed to an animal outside, curled up in a ball on one of the paths through the grounds. It was only a cat.

'I hate animals! I hate the countryside! It's full of creaking and snapping sounds that make me jump . . . At night – every night – there's an owl somewhere that gives ghastly hooting cries . . .'

The French windows seemed to frighten her as well, because she was staring at them as if she expected to see enemies pour through them from all sides.

'I will not sleep here alone in the house! I won't!'

'Is there a telephone?'

'No . . . My brother thought about getting one, but we cannot afford it. Can you imagine? Living in such a big house, with I don't know how many hectares, and not being able to pay for a telephone, or electricity or even a cleaning woman for the hard work! That's Carl all over! He's like his father . . .'

And she burst out laughing, but with an edge of hysteria.

It was a difficult situation, because she could not manage to compose herself and although she was still shaking with laughter, there was desperation in her eyes.

'What is it? What's so funny?'

'Nothing! You mustn't be angry with me . . . I'm thinking of when we were children, in our castle back home, with Carl's tutor and all the servants, the visitors, the carriages pulled by four horses . . . and *here* . . .'

Knocking over the tin of milk, she went to lean her forehead against a windowpane, staring out at the front steps baking in the sun.

'I'll arrange for a policeman to keep an eye on the house tonight.'

'Yes, good . . . No! I don't want a policeman, I want you to come yourself, chief inspector! Otherwise I'll be frightened . . .'

Was she laughing? Crying? She was panting: her entire body was trembling from head to toe.

She might have been putting on a show to make a fool of someone – but she might just as well have been on the verge of a breakdown.

'Don't leave me by myself!'

'I have work to do.'

'But if Carl has run away . . .'

'You think he's guilty?'

'I don't know! I don't know any more. If he has run off . . .'

'Do you want me to lock you in your room again?'

'No. What I want, as soon as possible, tomorrow

morning, is to get away from this house, from this cross-roads! I want to go to Paris, where the streets are full of people, where life goes on . . . The countryside scares me . . . I just don't know . . .'

And suddenly, 'Will they arrest Carl in Belgium?'

'There will be a warrant for his extradition.'

'It's unbelievable. When I think that only three days ago . . .'

She clasped her head in both hands, mussing her blonde hair.

Maigret stood outside on the front steps.

'I will see you later today, mademoiselle.'

He strode off with relief and yet he was sorry to leave her. Lucas was walking up and down the road.

'Anything new?'

'Nothing! The insurance agent came over to ask me if he was going to get a car back soon.'

Monsieur Michonnet had chosen to ask Lucas rather than Maigret. And they could see him in his little garden, watching them.

'He has nothing to keep himself busy?'

'He claims he can't visit his clients out in the country without a car. He's talking about suing us for damages.'

A van and a touring car carrying an entire family were waiting by the pumps at the garage.

'One fellow who's not working himself to death,' remarked the sergeant, 'is that Monsieur Oscar! He seems to earn money hand over fist. That place is hopping day and night . . .'

'Have you got any tobacco?'

The spring sunshine bathing the countryside was surprisingly strong, and Maigret mopped his brow.

'I'm going to nap for an hour,' he murmured. 'We'll see what happens tonight . . .'

Monsieur Oscar called out to him as he walked by.

'Take a drop, chief inspector? Just a quick one, since you're in the neighbourhood!'

'Some other time!'

Judging from the loud voices coming from the millstone villa, Michonnet was arguing with his wife.

6. Back from the Dead

It was five that afternoon when Maigret was awakened by Lucas bringing him a telegram from the Belgian police.

Isaac Goldberg under surveillance for several months as standard of living exceeded visible income Stop Suspected trafficking mainly stolen jewels Stop No proof Stop Trip to France coincided theft 2,000,000 in jewels London two weeks ago Stop Anonymous letter affirms jewels surfaced Antwerp where two international thieves seen spending freely Stop Believe Goldberg bought jewels then entered France to fence Stop Request description jewels Scotland Yard Stop

Still half-asleep, Maigret stuffed the telegram into his pocket and asked, 'Anything else?'

'No. I've kept an eye on the crossroads. When I saw the garage owner all dressed up I asked him where he was going. Seems he and his wife visit Paris once a week for dinner and a show. On those evenings they stay over in a hotel and return the next day.'

'Has he left?'

'By this time, he must have, yes!'

'You asked him which restaurant he was going to?'

'L'Escargot, Rue de la Bastille. Then he's off to the Théâtre de l'Ambigu and will stay at the Hôtel Rambuteau, Rue de Rivoli.'

'That about covers it,' muttered the inspector, who was combing his hair.

'The insurance fellow had his wife tell me that he'd like to talk to you, or rather, "have a chat with you", as he put it.'

'Nothing else?'

Maigret went into the kitchen, where the innkeeper's wife was preparing the evening meal. He cut himself a thick hunk of bread, moved on to a terrine of pâté, and asked for a mug of white wine.'

'You're not waiting for supper?'

The inspector began devouring his huge sandwich in reply.

The sergeant watched him, obviously eager to talk.

'You're expecting some important development tonight, is that it?'

'Humpf . . .'

But why deny it? Standing there eating, wasn't he like a soldier about to go into battle?

'I've been going over things,' began Lucas, 'trying to organize my ideas. It's not easy . . .'

Chewing away, Maigret looked placidly at his colleague.

'It's still the girl who puzzles me the most. At times I feel that everyone around her – garage owner, insurance man, Carl Andersen – is guilty, but not her. At other times I'd swear instead that she's the only poisonous thing here . . .'

There was a twinkle of amusement in the inspector's eyes that seemed to say, 'Keep going!'

'There are moments when she really does seem like a girl from an aristocratic family, but again, at others she reminds me of when I was with Vice. You know what I mean, those girls who coolly reel off the most outrageous nonsense in the world, as bold as brass! Yet the details are so disturbing that you just can't believe such a girl could make them up. So you fall for her story . . . But later you find an old novel under her pillow and discover that she got everything from that book . . . Women who lie as easily as they breathe, and maybe even wind up believing all those stories they tell!'

'That's it?'

'You think I'm wrong?'

'I have no idea!'

'Remember, I believe different things at different times, and mostly it's Carl Andersen who worries me. Imagine an intelligent, cultivated, well-bred man like him, running a gang . . .'

'We'll see him tonight!'

'Him? But he's crossed the border.'

'Well . . .'

'You think that . . .'

'That this business is a whole lot more complicated than you imagine, Lucas. And that we'd be better off concentrating on a few important elements instead of getting lost in details.

'For instance,' continued Maigret, 'Monsieur Michonnet was the first person to file a complaint and he's the one who wants me to go and see him this evening.

'An evening, in fact, when the garage owner will *quite obviously* be off in Paris!

'And where is Goldberg's Minerva? Think about that, too! As there aren't many of them in France, it's not an easy car to make disappear.'

'You think that Monsieur Oscar . . .'

'Not so fast! . . . But if you feel like it, play around with those three little things.'

'But what about Else?'

'Her again?'

And wiping his mouth, Maigret went out to the main road. Fifteen minutes later he rang the Michonnets' bell and was welcomed by the woman's surly face.

'My husband is waiting for you upstairs!'

'So good of him . . .'

Oblivious to the irony of his words, she led him upstairs. Michonnet was in his bedroom, seated in a low-slung Voltaire armchair near the window. The shade was pulled down and he had a tartan blanket tucked around his legs.

'Well, now!' he began aggressively. 'When will I be getting a car back? You think it's a good idea, do you, to deprive a man of his livelihood? And meanwhile, you're paying calls on that creature across the way, when you're not off having aperitifs with the garage owner! Fine police work that is! I'll not mince words with you, chief inspector! Yes, a fine state of affairs! Never mind the murderer! The top priority is to torment honest citizens! . . . I have a car: does it belong to me, yes or no? . . . I put it to you. Answer me! Is it mine? . . . Well, what gives you the right to keep my car locked up?'

'Are you ill?' Maigret asked quietly, looking at the blanket around the man's legs.

'Who wouldn't be! I'm fretting myself into an attack of gout! It always goes to my legs . . . I'm looking at two or three nights sitting sleepless in this chair. I asked you here to tell you this: look at the state I'm in! You can see for yourself that I'm unable to work, especially without a car! . . . Enough . . . I will call you as a witness when I sue for damages. And now, I bid you goodnight, monsieur!'

He had made his speech with the exaggerated bravado of a small-minded prig confident of being in the right.

'But while you seem to be skulking around spying on us,' added Madame Michonnet, 'the murderer himself is still out there! That's our justice! Attacking ordinary folks, but leaving the big shots free!'

'Is that all you have to say to me?'

Michonnet glared and sat back in his armchair while his wife led the way to the door.

The interior of the house was of a piece with its façade: spotless suites of furniture, gleaming with polish but seemingly frozen in place, unused.

Out in the corridor Maigret stopped at an old-fashioned wall-telephone and promptly turned the crank, as Madame Michonnet looked on in outrage.

'Hello, operator? This is the Police Judiciaire! Can you tell me if there have been any calls this afternoon for the Three Widows Crossroads? . . . There are two numbers, you say, the garage and the Michonnet villa? . . . Good, and when? . . . A call for the garage from Paris at around one o'clock and another towards five? . . . And the other number? . . . Only one call . . . From Paris? . . . At five past five? . . . Thank you, mademoiselle.'

His eyes alight with mischief, he bowed to Madame Michonnet.

'I wish you a pleasant evening, madame.'

He opened the gate of the Three Widows house with practised ease, walked around the back to the drawing room and on upstairs.

Else Andersen met him in a state of great agitation.

'I'm sorry to make such demands of you, chief inspector; you'll think I'm presumptuous, but I am so restless, on edge . . . I'm frightened and I don't know why! Ever since our conversation this morning I've felt that you are the only one who can protect me from harm . . . You now know this sinister crossroads as well as I do, these three houses that seem to defy one another . . . Do you believe in premonitions? I do, like all women – and I sense that something bad will happen before this night is over . . .'

'And you're asking me again to watch over you?'

'It's too much to ask, isn't it – but I can't help being afraid!'

Maigret's eye had been caught for a moment by a painting of a snowy landscape, which hung crookedly on a wall, but he turned immediately to the girl, who stood waiting for his reply.

'Aren't you afraid for your reputation?'

'What does that matter to someone who's frightened?'

'In that case, I will return in one hour. A few orders to give . . .'

'Really? You'll come back? That's a promise? . . . Besides,

I have all sorts of things to tell you, things I've remembered only in bits and pieces . . .'

'About?'

'My brother . . . But they may not be important . . . Well . . . For example, I remember, after that plane crash, the doctor taking care of him told Father that he could vouch for his patient's physical health, but not his mental health. I'd never really thought about what he meant . . . And other things . . . His insistence on living far from any city, hiding away . . . I'll tell you about all that when you return.'

She smiled at him with gratitude and only a flicker of lingering fear.

Walking past the millstone villa, Maigret looked up automatically at the first-floor window, which shone bright yellow in the darkness. Framed in the glowing shade was the silhouette of Monsieur Michonnet, sitting in his armchair.

At the inn, the inspector simply gave Lucas a few orders without any explanation.

'See to it that half a dozen inspectors are posted around the crossroads. Once an hour make sure that Monsieur Oscar is still in Paris by phoning the restaurant, then the theatre and the hotel. Have everyone who leaves any of the three houses here followed.'

'Where will you be?'

'At the Andersens' place.'

'You think that . . .'

'I don't think anything, old friend! I'll see you later, or tomorrow morning.'

Night had fallen. As he went back to the main road, the inspector made sure that his revolver was loaded and that he had sufficient tobacco.

The moustachioed profile of the insurance agent and the shadow of his armchair were still visible in the Michonnets' upstairs window.

Else Andersen had changed her black velvet dress for the peignoir she had worn that morning and Maigret found her stretched out on the divan, smoking a cigarette, calmer than he had last seen her but frowning thoughtfully.

'If you only knew how relieved I am to know you're here, chief inspector! Some people inspire confidence from the moment you meet them . . . but they are rare. In any case, I personally have met few people with whom I felt an instinctive, sympathetic bond . . . Do smoke, if you like . . .'

'Have you eaten?'

'I'm not hungry. I don't know any more what's keeping me going . . . For four days, from the horrible instant that body was found in the car, I've been thinking, thinking . . . Trying to understand, to make up my mind . . .'

'And you conclude that your brother is the guilty one?'

'No. I do not want to accuse Carl. Especially as, even if he actually were guilty, it would only be due to a moment of uncontrollable madness . . . You've chosen the worst armchair. If you would like to lie down at any point, there is a cot in the next room.'

She was calm and anxious at the same time. A seeming calm, deliberate, painfully achieved. An anxiety that still managed to surface at certain moments.

'Something terrible has already happened in this house, a long time ago, hasn't it? Carl has spoken about it, but only vaguely . . . He was afraid of frightening me. He always treats me like a little girl.'

Her whole body leaned forwards, in a supple movement, as she flicked her cigarette ash into the china bowl on the lacquered table. Her peignoir fell open, as it had that morning, revealing a small, round breast. Only for an instant. And yet Maigret had had time to notice a scar, and he frowned.

'You were wounded some time ago!'

'What do you mean?'

Blushing, she instinctively drew the edges of her peignoir closed over her chest.

'You have a scar on your right breast.'

She was deeply embarrassed.

'Excuse me,' she said. 'I'm used to dressing casually here, I never thought . . . As for that scar . . . There! Another thing I've suddenly recalled, but it's certainly just a coincidence . . . When we were still children, Carl and I used to play on the castle grounds and I remember that one day he was given a rifle, for Saint Nicholas's Day. Carl must have been fourteen . . . It's all so silly, you'll see. At first he shot at a target. After an evening at the circus, the next day he wanted to play at being William Tell. I held out a cardboard target in each hand. The first bullet hit me in the chest.'

Maigret had stood up. He walked over to the divan with a face so impassive that Else grew uneasy as he approached, and she clutched the neck of her peignoir.

But he was not looking at her. He was staring at the wall behind the divan, where the snowy landscape painting was now perfectly level.

Slowly he swung the frame to one side and discovered a niche in the wall, neither large nor deep, where two bricks had been removed. Within the niche were an automatic loaded with six bullets, a box of cartridges, a key and a tube of veronal.

Else had watched his every move but seemed hardly to react at all. A slight rosiness in the cheeks; her eyes a bit more bright . . .

'I would probably have got around to showing you that hiding place myself, chief inspector . . .'

'Really?'

As he spoke he was pocketing the revolver and noting that half the veronal tablets in the tube were gone. He went over to the bedroom door and stuck the key into the lock: it fitted perfectly.

The young woman had risen from the divan. She no longer cared about covering her chest and moved her hands awkwardly and abruptly as she spoke.

'What you just discovered confirms what I've already told you, but you must understand my position! How could I accuse my brother? . . . If I had confessed to you, when you first came here, that I have for a long time now considered him insane, you would have been shocked by my behaviour. And yet, it's the truth . . .'

Her accent, which grew stronger whenever she became emotional, imparted a peculiar quality to every word she said.

'The revolver?'

'How can I explain . . . We left Denmark as paupers, but my brother was convinced that, with his education, he would find a brilliant position in Paris . . . He did not. And became even more distressingly strange. When he resolved to bury us out here, I understood that he was seriously ill. Especially as he insisted on locking me in my bedroom every night under the pretext that enemies might attack us! You can imagine my situation, imprisoned within these walls, unable to escape in case of fire, for example, or any other catastrophe . . . I couldn't sleep! I was as frantic as if I'd been underground in a tunnel . . .

'One day when he was in Paris, I had a locksmith come to make me a key to the bedroom door. Since I was locked in here, I had to climb out of the bedroom window . . .

'Now I could move around freely, but it wasn't enough. There were days when Carl was half mad . . . He often talked about destroying us both to avoid complete ruin.

'I bought a revolver in Arpajon on another day when my brother was in Paris. And as I was sleeping poorly, I got myself some veronal.

'You see how simple it is! He's so distrustful . . . No one is more wary than a deranged man who's still lucid enough to realize that he is disturbed . . . I made this hiding place one night.'

'Is that it?'

She was surprised by his brutal bluntness.

'Don't you believe me?'

Without answering, he went to the window, opened it,

then the shutters – and was bathed in the cool freshness of the night.

The road below was like a stream of ink that shone as if by moonlight whenever cars went by. The headlamps would gleam in the distance, perhaps ten kilometres away. Then suddenly there'd be a sort of cyclone, a roaring whoosh of air, a single red tail light fading into the darkness.

The petrol pumps were lit up. In the Michonnets' villa, one light still outlined the silhouette of the insurance agent in his armchair on the pale blind upstairs.

'Close the window, chief inspector!'

Maigret turned around. He saw Else shivering, drawing her peignoir tightly around her.

'Do you understand now why I'm worried? You've persuaded me to tell you everything – but I wouldn't want anything to happen to Carl, not for the world! He's told me many times that we would die together . . .'

'Would you please be quiet!'

He was straining to hear the noises of the night, so he drew his armchair over to the window and put his feet up on the railing.

'But I'm cold, I tell you . . .'

'Put some clothes on!'

'You don't believe me?'

'Be quiet, dammit!'

And he began smoking. Vague sounds came from a distant farm: a lowing cow, shifting, indistinct noises of movement . . . Off in the garage, though, as steel objects were banged about, the electric tyre-pump began vibrating.

'And I trusted you! . . . But now—'

'Once and for all, are you going to be quiet?'

He had spotted a shadow behind a tree by the road, close to the house, and assumed it was one of the inspectors he had requested.

'I'm hungry . . .'

He turned around angrily to face the young woman, who looked pathetic.

'Go and get something to eat!'

'I don't dare go; I'm afraid . . .'

Maigret shrugged, made sure that everything was quiet outside and abruptly decided to go downstairs. He knew his way around the kitchen. Near the stove were some leftover cold meat, bread and part of a bottle of beer.

He took everything upstairs and placed it on the lacquered table, near the cigarette bowl.

'You're being mean to me, chief inspector.'

She looked like such a little girl . . . She seemed about to burst into tears!

'I don't have time to be mean or nice. Eat!'

'You're not hungry? . . . Are you angry that I told you the truth?'

But he was already turning his back on her to look out of the window. Behind the shade, Madame Michonnet was bending over her husband, probably giving him some medicine, for she was holding a spoon to his face.

Else had picked up a piece of cold veal with her fingertips and now nibbled on it glumly. Then she poured herself a glass of beer.

'It tastes terrible!' she exclaimed, and gasped convulsively.

'But why won't you close that window? I'm scared . . . Don't you ever feel sorry for people?'

Exasperated, Maigret suddenly shut the window and looked over at Else like a man about to lose his temper.

Then he saw her turn white, saw her blue eyes glaze over and her hand reach out for some support . . . He reached her just in time to slip an arm around her waist as she collapsed.

He lowered her gently to the floor, raised her eyelids to check her pupils and sniffed the empty glass, which had an acrid smell.

There was a spoon on the table. He used it to pry Else's jaws open and immediately thrust the spoon into her mouth, repeatedly touching it to her palate and the back of her throat.

Her face twitched a few times. Her chest heaved in spasms.

She was lying on the rug. Tears trickled from beneath her eyelids, and when her head fell to one side, she was shaken by a huge hiccup.

The contractions caused by the spoon were clearing her stomach: a yellowish liquid stained the rug; some drops glistened on her peignoir.

Taking the water pitcher from the dressing table, Maigret moistened her face.

He kept turning impatiently towards the window.

And Else was taking a long time to come around. She moaned weakly. Finally she raised her head.

'What . . . ?'

She got to her feet, disoriented and still shaky, and saw the spoon, the empty glass, the stained rug.

Then she began sobbing, her head in her hands.

'You see, I was right to be afraid: they've tried to poison me! And you didn't want to believe me . . . You—'

She started at the same instant as Maigret. Both of them froze for a few moments, listening intently.

A shot had been fired near the house, probably in the garden, and been followed by a hoarse cry.

Now a long, shrill whistle was sounding over by the road. People were running. Someone was shaking the front gate. Through the window Maigret could see his inspectors' flashlights searching in the darkness. Not quite a hundred metres away, in the villa's window, Madame Michonnet was settling a pillow behind her husband's head . . .

The inspector opened the bedroom door. He heard noise below.

Then Lucas yelled up the stairs: 'Chief!'

'Who was it?'

'Carl Andersen . . . He isn't dead . . . Are you coming?'

Maigret turned and saw Else sitting hunched on the edge of the divan with her elbows on her knees, staring straight ahead, with her chin cupped in her hands and her jaws clenched. She was shivering uncontrollably.

7. The Two Wounds

Carl Andersen was carried up to his bedroom. An inspector followed, bringing the lamp from the drawing room. The wounded man neither moved nor groaned. Only after he had been laid on his bed did Maigret lean over him and see that his eyes were half open.

Andersen recognized him, seemed somewhat comforted and reached for the inspector's hand, murmuring, 'Else?'

She was standing in the doorway in an attitude of anxious waiting, looking bleakly into the bedroom.

It was a striking tableau. Carl had lost his black monocle, and next to the healthy but blood shot, half-closed eye, the glass one still stared vacantly.

The glow of the oil lamp made everything seem mysterious. The police could be heard searching the grounds and raking the gravelled paths.

As for Else, when Maigret told her firmly to go over to her brother, she went rigid and hardly dared advance towards him at all.

'I think he's badly wounded,' whispered Lucas.

She must have heard. She looked at him but hesitated to go any closer to her brother, who gazed at her intently, struggling to sit up in bed.

In a sudden storm of tears, she turned and ran to her

own room, where she threw herself, weeping, on to the divan.

Maigret motioned to the sergeant to keep an eye on her and attended to the wounded man, removing Andersen's jacket and waistcoat with the ease of someone familiar with this sort of incident.

'Don't be afraid . . . We've sent for a doctor. Else is in her room.'

Andersen was silent, like someone crushed by some mysterious misgiving. He looked around him as if he were anxious to resolve an enigma or discover a solemn secret.

'Later on I will question you, but—'

Examining the man's bare torso, the inspector frowned.

'You've been shot twice . . . This wound in your back is far from fresh . . .'

And it was a terrible injury: ten square centimetres of skin had been torn away. The flesh was literally cut up, burned, swollen, encrusted with scabs of dried blood. This wound had stopped bleeding, which showed that it was a few hours old, whereas the latest bullet had fractured the left shoulder blade. As Maigret was cleaning the wound, the deformed bullet spilled out of it.

He picked it up. The bullet was not from a revolver, but from a rifle, like the one that had killed Madame Goldberg.

'Where is Else?' murmured the wounded man, who was bearing his pain without grimacing.

'In her room. Don't move . . . Did you see who just shot you?'

'No.'

'And the other shooter? Where was that?'

Andersen frowned, opened his mouth to speak, but gave up, exhausted. With a faint motion of his left arm he tried to explain that he could not talk any more.

'Well, doctor?'

It was irritating trying to function in the semi-darkness. There were only two oil lamps in the house, one currently in the wounded man's bedroom, the other in Else's.

Downstairs, one candle burned, without lighting even a quarter of the drawing room.

'Unless there are unexpected complications, he'll pull through. The first wound is the more serious one. He must have received it early in the afternoon, if not late this morning. A bullet from a Browning fired point-blank into the back. Absolutely point-blank! I even think it possible that the muzzle of the weapon was right against the flesh. The victim made a sudden movement, deflecting the shot, so the ribs are basically all that were hit. Bruises on the shoulder, the arms, some scratches on the hands and knees – these must have occurred at the same time . . .'

'And the other bullet?'

'The shoulder blade is shattered. He must be seen to by a surgeon tomorrow. I can give you the address of a clinic in Paris . . . There is one in the area, but if the wounded man can afford it, I recommend Paris.'

'Was he able to get about after the first incident?'

'Probably . . . No vital organ was hit . . . It would have been a question of stamina, of will-power. Although I do fear that he'll have a stiff shoulder for the rest of his life.'

The police had found nothing out in the grounds, but they had taken up positions so as to be ready for a thorough search at first light.

Maigret then went to check on Andersen, who was relieved to see him.

'Else?'

'In her bedroom, I've already told you twice.'

'Why . . .'

Always that morbid anxiety, betrayed by the man's twitching face and by his every glance.

'Do you know of any enemies you might have?'

'No.'

'Don't upset yourself. Simply tell me how you got shot that first time. Go slowly . . . Take it easy . . .'

'I was on my way to Dumas and Son . . .'

'You didn't get there.'

'I tried! At the Porte d'Orléans, a man signalled to me to pull over.'

Andersen asked for some water and drained a large glass, then looked up at the ceiling and continued.

'He told me he was a policeman. He even showed me a card, which I didn't really look at. He ordered me to drive across Paris and take the road to Compiègne, claiming that I was going to be brought face to face with a witness. He got into the passenger seat beside me.'

'What did he look like?'

'Tall, wearing a grey fedora. Shortly before Compiègne, the main road goes through a forest. At a turning, I felt a violent impact on my back . . . A hand grabbed the steering wheel from me while I was pushed out of the car. I lost consciousness. I came to in the roadside ditch. The car was gone.'

'What time was it?'

'Perhaps eleven in the morning . . . I'm not sure. The clock in my car doesn't work. I walked into the forest, to recover from the shock and have time to think. I was having dizzy spells . . . I heard trains going by . . . Finally I came to a small station. By five o'clock I was in Paris, where I got a room. There I took care of myself, brushed off my clothes . . . And I came here.'

'In secret . . .'

'Yes.'

'Why?'

'I don't know.'

'Did you meet anyone?'

'No! I avoided the main road and came in through the grounds . . . Just as I reached the front steps, the shot rang out . . . I'd like to see Else.'

'Do you know that someone has tried to poison her?'

Maigret was completely unprepared for Andersen's reaction to his words. The wounded man sat up all by himself, stared eagerly at the inspector and stammered, 'Really?'

He seemed overjoyed, released from a nightmare.

'Oh! I want to see her!'

Maigret went out into the hall to fetch Else, who was in her room, lying on the divan with empty eyes. Lucas was watching her sullenly.

'Would you come with me?'

'What did he say?'

She was still frightened, uncertain. After taking a few

hesitant steps into the wounded man's room, she rushed over and hugged him, talking to him in Danish.

A gloomy Lucas was watching Maigret out of the corner of his eye.

'Can you figure any of this out?'

Instead of replying, the inspector shrugged and began issuing orders.

'Make sure that the garage owner has not left Paris . . . Telephone the Préfecture, have them send out a surgeon first thing in the morning . . . Even tonight, if possible.'

'Where are you going?'

'No idea . . . As for the surveillance around the grounds: keep it up, but don't expect anything.'

Maigret went downstairs, down the front steps, out to the main road, alone. The garage was closed, but the milky-white globes of the pumps were shining.

The light was on upstairs at the Michonnet villa. Behind the shade, the insurance agent's silhouette was still in the same place.

The night was cool. A thin mist was drifting up from the fields, forming into waves about a metre above the ground. From over towards Arpajon came the increasingly loud sounds of an engine and clanking metal; five minutes later, a lorry pulled up at the garage, honking its horn.

A small door opened in the iron security shutter, revealing an electric light bulb burning inside the garage.

'Twenty litres!'

The sleepy mechanic worked the pump; the driver stayed high up in his cab. The chief inspector walked over, his hands in his pockets, his pipe between his teeth.

'Monsieur Oscar not back yet?'

'What? You here? . . . Well, no! When he goes to Paris, he only comes back the next morning.'

A moment's hesitation, then: 'Say, Arthur, you'd best pick up your spare: it's ready . . .'

And the mechanic fetched a wheel with its tyre from the garage, rolling it out and laboriously attaching it to the back of the lorry.

The vehicle drove off. Its red tail light dwindled into the distance. The mechanic yawned and sighed.

'Still looking for the murderer? At this hour? . . . Well, me, if I could just snooze my fill, I swear I wouldn't care one way or the other!'

A bell tower struck two o'clock. A train trailed sparks along the horizon.

'You coming in? . . . Or not?'

And the man stretched, impatient to get back to sleep.

Maigret went inside, looked at the whitewashed walls, where red inner tubes and tyres of every brand, most of them in bad shape, were hanging from nails.

'Tell me! What's he going to do with the wheel you gave him?'

'Huh? . . . Why, put it on his lorry, of course!'

'You think so? . . . It'll drive lopsided, his lorry, because that wheel hasn't the same diameter as the others . . .'

The mechanic began to look worried.

'Just a minute now . . . Maybe I mistook the wheel . . . Did I go and give him the one from old man Mathieu's van?'

There was a loud explosion: Maigret had just shot at

one of the inner tubes hanging on the wall. And along with the escaping air, small white paper packets came pouring out of the collapsing tube.

'Don't move, you little rat!'

For the mechanic, bent over, was about to run at him head first.

'Watch it, or I'll shoot.'

'What do you want from me?'

'Hands up! . . . Now!'

He stepped smartly over to Jojo, patted his pockets and confiscated a fully loaded revolver.

'Go and lie down on your cot.'

Maigret pushed the door shut with his foot. One look at the mechanic's freckled face was enough to tell him that the fellow would not give up easily.

'Lie down.'

Glancing around, he saw no rope but spotted a coil of electric wire.

'Your hands!'

Realizing that Maigret would have to put down his revolver, the mechanic tensed for action, but got punched right in the face. His nose bled. His lip swelled up. The man growled in rage. Then his hands were tied and soon his feet as well.

'How old are you?'

'Twenty-one.'

'Released from where?'

Silence.

All Maigret had to do was make a fist.

'The reformatory at Montpellier.'

'That's better! And do you know what's in those little packets?'

The reply was a snarl: 'Drugs!'

The mechanic was flexing his muscles, trying to snap the wire bonds.

'What was in the spare tyre?'

'Don't know.'

'Then why did you give it to that driver rather than another?'

'I'm not talking any more!'

'Too bad for you!'

Five inner tubes were punctured one after another, but they did not all contain cocaine. Under a patch that had covered a long slit in one tube, Maigret found silverware stamped with the coronet of a marquis. Another tube held lace and some antique jewellery.

There were ten cars in the garage. Maigret tried to start each engine, but only one would work. So, armed with a monkey wrench backed up by a hammer, he got busy taking apart engines and cutting open petrol tanks.

The mechanic watched him with a mocking smile.

'Can't say we're short on the goods!' he sneered.

The tank in a four-horse-power car was crammed full of bearer bonds worth at least 300,000 francs.

'Is this the haul from the break-in at that big savings and loan company?'

'Could be!'

'And these old coins?'

'Dunno.'

There was more variety than in the back room of a second-hand shop. Everything imaginable: pearls, bank-notes, American currency, official stamps and seals that must have been used to forge passports.

Maigret was unable to search everywhere, but when he tore open the worn-out cushions of a sedan, he found still more: silver florins, which convinced him that everything in that garage was more than met the eye.

A lorry swept past on the main road. Fifteen minutes later, another went by without stopping, and the inspector frowned.

He was beginning to see how the business was run. The garage was a no-account place along the main road, fifty kilometres from Paris, not far from some big provincial cities such as Chartres, Orléans, Le Mans, Châteaudun.

No neighbours, aside from those living in the Three Widows house and the Michonnet villa.

What could they see? A thousand cars going by every day. At least a hundred of them stopped at the petrol pumps. A few would go in for repairs. The garage sold or changed tyres and wheels. Cans of oil and drums of diesel oil came and went.

One detail was especially interesting. Big lorries headed for Paris drove by every evening, delivering vegetables to Les Halles. Later that night or in the morning, they came back empty.

Empty? Weren't they the ones ferrying stolen merchandise in the baskets and crates of produce?

The enterprise could well be a regular, even daily event. A single tyre, the one concealing cocaine, was enough to show the extent of the trafficking, because that drug shipment was worth over 200,000 francs.

What's more, didn't the garage repaint and disguise stolen cars? No witnesses! Monsieur Oscar in the doorway, hands in his pockets. Mechanics working with monkey wrenches or blowtorches. The five red-and-white petrol pumps providing an innocent front . . .

The butcher, the baker, the tourists: didn't they stop by here like everyone else?

A bell rang in the distance. Maigret checked his watch. It was half past three.

'Who's your boss?' he asked, without looking at his prisoner.

The man just smiled.

'You know you'll wind up talking . . . Is it Monsieur Oscar? What's his real name?'

'Oscar!'

The mechanic was practically giggling.

'Did Monsieur Goldberg come here?'

'Who's that?'

'You'd know better than I! The Belgian who was murdered . . .'

'No kidding!'

'Whose job was it to knock off the Danish fellow on the Compiègne road?'

'Somebody got knocked off?'

No doubt about it: Maigret's first impression was

panning out. He was up against a well-organized professional gang. And he soon had more proof. He heard a car
coming, then a screech of brakes as it stopped outside the
iron shutter. The horn sounded urgently.

Maigret rushed to the door, but before he could open
it, the car sped away so fast he could not even guess its
model.

Clenching his fists, he went back to the mechanic.

'How did you warn him off?'

'Me?'

And the fellow chuckled, holding up his wrists in their
wire bonds.

'Talk!'

'Must be that it smells fishy here and that driver's got a
good nose . . .'

Now Maigret was worried. He overturned the cot
roughly, sending Jojo sprawling, and looked for a possible
switch for a warning signal outside.

He found nothing under the bed, however. He left the
man lying on the floor, went outside and saw the five
pumps lit up as usual.

He was beginning to get really angry.

'There's no phone in the garage?'

'Go and take a look!'

'You do know you'll talk in the end . . .'

'I can't hear you!'

There was nothing more to be got from Jojo, a perfect
example of a confident, experienced criminal. For a quarter of an hour, Maigret walked up and down fifty metres

of the main road, searching without success for some possible signal.

The upstairs light at the Michonnet villa had been turned off. Only the Three Widows house was still lit, and the presence of the policemen surrounding the property was discreetly felt.

A limousine barrelled past.

'What kind of car does your boss have?'

To the east, dawn announced itself with a whitish haze that barely cleared the horizon.

Maigret studied the mechanic's hands. They were not touching anything that might have sent a signal.

A current of cool air came in through the little door standing open in the corrugated iron shutter over the garage.

Hearing the sound of an engine, Maigret started to go out to the road, but just as he noticed the approach of an open four-seater touring car, which wasn't doing more than thirty kilometres an hour and seemed about to pull in, the car exploded with gunfire.

Several men were shooting and bullets were rattling against the iron shutter.

Nothing could be seen except the glare of the headlights and the immobile shadows – heads, rather – just showing above the body of the car. Then came the roar of the accelerator . . .

Some broken windows . . . on the upper floor of the Three Widows house. The men in the car had kept shooting as they'd gone past.

Maigret had thrown himself flat on the ground and now stood up, his mouth dry, his pipe gone out.

He was certain: Monsieur Oscar had been driving the car that had just plunged back into the darkness.

8. Missing Persons

Before the chief inspector even had time to get out on to the road, a taxi raced up and slammed on its brakes in front of the petrol pumps. A man jumped out – and collided with Maigret.

'Grandjean!' exclaimed the chief inspector.

'Petrol, quick!'

The taxi driver was a nervous wreck, because he'd been speeding at over a hundred kilometres an hour in a car meant to do eighty at most.

Grandjean belonged to the highway patrol; there were two other inspectors in the taxi with him, and each man gripped a revolver in both fists.

The petrol tank was filled with feverish haste.

'How far ahead are they?'

'About five kilometres . . .'

The driver was waiting to take off again.

'You stay here!' Maigret ordered Grandjean. 'The other two will continue on without you.

'Don't take any risks!' he advised them. 'No matter what happens, we've got them. Tail them, that's all . . .'

The taxi set out. A sagging mudguard made a racket all down the road.

'Let's hear it, Grandjean . . .'

And Maigret heard him out, all the while keeping an

eye on Jojo and the three houses and listening intently to the noises of the night.

'It was Lucas who telephoned me, told me to watch the owner of this place, Monsieur Oscar . . . I began following him at Porte d'Orléans. They had a big dinner at L'Escargot, where they spoke to no one, then went on to L'Ambigu . . . Until then, nothing to report. At midnight, they come out of the theatre and I see them head for the Chope Saint-Martin . . . You know the place; in the little dining room upstairs, there are always a few tough guys . . . So Monsieur Oscar walks in like he owns the joint. The waiters welcome him, the proprietor shakes his hand, asks him how business is going . . .

'As for the wife, her, she's right at home there too.

'They sit down at a table where there were already three guys and a tart. I recognized one of the guys, he owns a bar somewhere around République. The second had a junkshop, Rue du Temple. As for the third guy, I don't know, but the tart with him has got to be on record with Vice . . .

'They start drinking champagne, having a gay old time. Then they order crayfish, onion soup, what have you, a real blowout, like those people get up to: yelling, slapping their thighs, belting out a little song now and then . . .

'There was one jealous scene, because Monsieur Oscar was cuddling too close to the tart and his wife didn't care for her. That worked out in the end, thanks to a fresh bottle of champagne.

'Time to time, the *patron* came over to have a drink with his customers and he even stood them a round. Then, towards three o'clock, I think, the waiter arrived to say Monsieur Oscar's wanted on the phone.

'When he came back from the booth, he wasn't laughing any more. He gave me a dirty look, because I was the only one there they didn't know. He spoke in a low voice to the others . . . They were in some kind of mess! They pulled the longest faces . . . The girl – I mean Monsieur Oscar's wife – had circles under her eyes and halfway down her cheeks and was drinking like mad to give herself some Dutch courage . . .

'There was only one guy who left with the couple, the fellow I didn't know, some kind of Italian or Spaniard . . .

'While they were saying goodnight and all that I got out ahead of them to the boulevard. I picked a taxi that didn't look too dilapidated and called two inspectors on duty over at Porte Saint-Denis.

'You saw their car . . . Well! They started going like blazes at Boulevard Saint-Michel. They were whistled down at least ten times, never even looked back. We had real trouble following them. The taxi driver – a Russian – claimed I was making him burn out his engine . . .'

'They're the ones who were shooting?'

'Yes!'

After hearing all the gunfire, Lucas had left the Three Widows house and now joined the inspector.

'What's going on?' he asked.

'How's the patient?'

'Weaker. I think he'll make it till morning, though. The surgeon should arrive soon. But what happened here?'

Lucas took in the garage's iron shutter, scarred by

bullets, and the cot where the mechanic was still tied up with electric wire.

'An organized gang, then, chief?'

'And how!'

Maigret was unusually worried; it was the slight hunching of his shoulders that gave it away. His lips were clamped hard around the stem of his pipe.

'Lucas, you organize the dragnet. Phone Arpajon, Étampes, Chartres, Orléans, Le Mans, Rambouillet . . . You'd best take a look at the map . . . I want every police station on alert! Get the roadblock chains up outside the towns . . . We've got them, this bunch . . . What's Else Andersen doing?'

'I don't know. I left her in her room. She's very depressed.'

'You don't say!' barked Maigret with surprising sarcasm.

They were still standing out in the road.

'Where should I call from?'

'There's a phone in the hall of the garage owner's house. Start with Orléans, because they've probably gone through Étampes by now.'

A light came on in an isolated farmhouse surrounded by fields. The family was getting up. A lantern disappeared around the end of a wall, and then the windows of a stable lit up.

'Five o'clock . . . They're beginning to milk the cows.'

Lucas went off to force open the door of Monsieur Oscar's house with a crowbar from the garage.

As for Grandjean, he followed Maigret around without really understanding what was happening.

'The latest incidents are as clear as day,' grumbled the

inspector. 'All we need to find out is what started it all . . .

'Look! Up there is a citizen who sent for me specifically to show me that he couldn't walk. He's been sitting in the same place for hours, without moving a muscle, not one muscle . . .

'Aha! Michonnet's windows are lit up, aren't they! And there I was, just now, looking for the signal! You can't understand the problem now . . . The traffic was going on by without stopping! But all that time, the bedroom window *was completely dark . . .*'

Maigret laughed like someone tickled pink.

And suddenly his colleague saw him pull a revolver from his pocket and aim it at an unbroken upstairs window, at the shadow of a head leaning back in an armchair.

The report was as sharp as a whip-crack. Then came the shattering of the window and a shower of glass shards into the garden.

Yet nothing moved in the bedroom. The shadow was intact behind the linen shade.

'What have you done?'

'Break down the door! . . . No – ring the bell instead! I'd be surprised if someone didn't open up.'

But no one did. The house was completely silent.

'Break it down!'

Grandjean was a big, burly man. He reared back and threw himself three times at the door, which finally gave way, ripped off its hinges.

'Careful . . . Easy does it . . .'

They each had a weapon out. The first light they turned

on was in the dining room. On the table, still sitting on the red check cloth, were dirty dinner dishes and a carafe with some white wine left in it. Maigret finished it off, right from the carafe.

There was nothing in the drawing room. Dust covers on furniture. The musty atmosphere of a room no one ever uses.

A cat was the only creature to run out of the white-tiled kitchen.

Grandjean kept looking uneasily at Maigret. They soon went upstairs to the landing and its three closed doors.

The inspector opened the one to the front bedroom.

The shade was stirring in a draught from the broken window. They saw a ridiculous object leaning against the armchair: a broom with a round turban of rags around the top, which stuck up over the back of the chair so it would look like a head in the shadow seen from outside.

But this sight did not amuse Maigret, who opened a connecting door and turned on the light in the neighbouring bedroom, which was empty.

The third door led to the attic. Apples lay on the floor, about two fingers' width apart from one another, and strings of green beans hung from a beam. There was a bedroom intended for a maid but unused, for it contained nothing but an old night table.

They went back downstairs. Maigret walked through the kitchen and out to the courtyard, which faced east, where the smudged halo of dawn was growing larger.

A small shed . . . A door that moved . . .

'Who's there?' he bellowed, brandishing his revolver.

There was a yelp of fright. No longer held from the inside, the door swung open, revealing a woman who fell to her knees.

'I haven't done anything! . . . I'm sorry! I . . . I . . .'

It was Madame Michonnet, her hair all mussed, her clothing flecked with plaster from the shed.

'Your husband?'

'I don't know! I swear I don't know anything! I'm so miserable, it's not fair . . .'

She was weeping. Her whole plump body seemed to soften and collapse. Her face had aged ten years, puffy from tears, sagging with fear.

'It wasn't me! I didn't do a thing! It's that man, across the way . . .'

'What man?'

'The foreigner . . . I know nothing about it, but he's the one, you can be sure of that! My husband isn't a murderer, or a thief . . . He's been honest all his life . . . It's him – with his bad eye! An evil eye! Ever since he came to the cross-roads, everything's been going wrong . . . I . . .'

The chicken run was full of white hens pecking at some fat yellow grains of corn strewn on the ground. The cat was perched on a window-sill, its eyes gleaming in the semi-darkness.

'Stand up.'

'What are you going to do to me? Who fired a gun?'

It was pathetic. She was fifty years old and crying like a child. She was so utterly at a loss that when she got to her feet and Maigret automatically gave her shoulder a little pat, she almost threw herself into his arms, resting her head against his chest, in any case, and clinging to his jacket lapels.

'I'm only a poor woman,' she moaned. 'I've worked all my life! When I got married, I was the cashier in the biggest hotel in Montpellier . . .'

Maigret eased her away from him but couldn't stem her lamentation.

'I should have stayed where I was . . . Because I was a valued employee . . . When I left, I remember that the hotel manager – who thought quite highly of me – told me that one day I would be sorry . . .

'And it's true! I've worked harder than I ever had before . . .'

She broke down again. The sight of her cat brought fresh distress.

'Poor Kitty! You're not to blame for any of this, either! And my hens, my furniture, my little house! . . . Inspector, you know I think I could kill that man if he were right here! I felt it the first day I saw him – just the sight of that black eye of his . . .'

'Where is your husband?'

'How would I know?'

'He went out early yesterday evening, didn't he? As soon as I left here. He wasn't any more laid up than I am . . .'

Stumped for a reply, she looked frantically around as if for help.

'He actually does suffer from gout . . .'

'Has Mademoiselle Else ever been here?'

'Never!' she exclaimed indignantly. 'I won't have such creatures in my home.'

'How about Monsieur Oscar?'

'Have you arrested him?'

'Almost!'

'It would serve him right, too . . . My husband should never have mixed with people who aren't our sort, who have no education. Oh, if only men listened to women! What do you think will happen? Tell me! I keep hearing gunshots . . . If something happens to Michonnet, I believe I'll die of shame! And besides, I'm too old to return to work . . .'

'Get back into the house.'

'What should I do?'

'Have a hot drink and wait. Get some sleep, if you can.'

'Sleep?'

And the word released another flood of frantic tears, which she had to deal with by herself, however, for both men had left.

Maigret went back to the house, though, and unhooked the phone receiver.

'Hello, Arpajon? . . . Police! . . . Would you tell me what numbers were requested during the night by this line?'

He had to wait for a few minutes. At last, the answer came: 'Archives 27-45 . . . It's a big café near Porte Saint-Martin . . .'

'I know,' said Maigret. 'Did you have other calls from the Three Widows Crossroads?'

'Just a moment ago, from the garage, requesting various police stations . . .'

'Thanks!'

When Maigret rejoined Inspector Grandjean out on the

road, a rain as fine as mist was beginning to fall, yet the sky was brightening to a milky white.

'Can you figure any of this out, chief?'

'I'm getting there . . .'

'That woman is faking it, isn't she?'

'She is perfectly sincere.'

'But . . . her husband . . .'

'Now, him, he's a different story. An honest man gone bad. Or, if you prefer, a crook who was born to be an honest man. There's nothing more complicated than that kind! They stew for hours trying to find a way out of trouble, coming up with incredible plots, playing their parts to perfection . . . Listen, what's still a mystery is what, for instance, made him decide at some point to turn crooked, so to speak. And we still need to find out what in heaven's name he was up to last night.'

And filling his pipe, the inspector went over to the front gate of the Three Widows house. An officer was standing guard.

'Any news?'

'I don't think we've found anything. We've surrounded the grounds. No one's been spotted, though.'

Maigret and Grandjean walked around the house, which was recovering its yellow colour in the half-light, its architectural details just beginning to emerge from the gloom.

The drawing room had not changed at all from Maigret's first visit: the easel still held the sketch of a fabric design with large crimson flowers. Two symmetrical reflections in the shape of an hourglass gleamed on a record on the phonograph. The dawning day was filtering into the room like wisps of fog.

The same step creaked on the staircase. In his room, Carl Andersen had been groaning before the inspector appeared but fell silent when he saw him. Mastering his pain, if not his anxiety, he stammered, 'Where is Else?'

'In her room.'

'Ah!'

Seemingly reassured, he sighed and felt his shoulder, frowning thoughtfully.

'I don't think I'm going to die from this . . .'

It was his glass eye that was most painful to see, because it played no part in the life of his face, remaining separate, clear and wide open while all the facial muscles were moving.

'I'd rather she did not see me like this. Do you think my shoulder will recover? Will a good surgeon be coming?'

Like Madame Michonnet, he was reduced to a child in his anguish. His eyes were pleading. He was asking to be reassured. What seemed to concern him the most, however, was the damage that his injuries might do to his appearance.

On the other hand he was displaying extraordinary will-power, a remarkable capacity for rising above his suffering. Maigret, who had seen his two wounds, knew what he was going through.

'Tell Else . . .'

'You don't want to see her?'

'No. I had better not. But tell her that I am here, that I will recover, that . . . I am perfectly lucid, that she should have confidence, have faith. Repeat that word to her: faith! Tell her to read a few verses in the Bible: the story of Job, for example . . . That makes you smile, because the French don't know the Bible well. Faith! . . . *And I shall always know my own* . . . God is speaking . . . God who knows his own . . . Tell her that! Also: *There will be more joy in heaven over one sinner* . . . She'll understand. And *The just man is tested nine times in a day* . . .'

It was astonishing. Wounded, in pain, bedridden under police guard, he was serenely quoting Holy Scripture.

'Faith! You will tell her, won't you? Because the only true example is innocence.'

He scowled. He had caught a fleeting smile on Grandjean's face. And between his teeth, he muttered to himself, *'Franzose!'*

Frenchman . . . In other words, unbeliever! Sceptic, freethinker, recreant, apostate!

Discouraged, he turned his face to the wall and stared at it with his one good eye.

'Tell her . . .'

Except that when Maigret and his colleague pushed open the door of Else's room, no one was there.

A hothouse atmosphere. An opaque cloud of aromatic tobacco smoke. And a feminine presence overwhelming enough to infatuate a schoolboy or even a grown man . . .

But not a living soul! The window was closed: Else had not left that way.

The painting hiding the niche in the wall, the tube of veronal, the key and the revolver was in its place . . .

Maigret slid it to one side. The revolver was missing.

'Stop looking at me like that, dammit!' exclaimed Maigret, glaring angrily at Grandjean, who was standing at his heels, gazing at him in beatific admiration.

Then the inspector bit down on his pipe so hard that he snapped the stem and sent the bowl rolling along the rug.

'She's run off?'

'Shut up!'

He was furious, out of line. Shocked, Grandjean did his best to stand perfectly still.

Day had not yet broken; that grey mist still drifted along the ground but brought no light. The baker's car drove by on the road, an old Ford with front wheels that wobbled along the asphalt.

Suddenly Maigret dashed to the hallway and down the stairs. And at the very moment when he reached the drawing room, where the French windows were standing open to the grounds, there was a ghastly cry, a death cry, the wavering howl of a beast in agony.

It was a woman crying out, her voice half stifled in some mysterious way.

It was far away or quite close by. It could have come from the eaves. It could have come from beneath the ground.

And it spread such anguish that the man on guard at the gate came running up, his face haggard.

'Chief inspector! Did you hear that?'

'Silence, damn it all!' shouted Maigret, at the absolute end of his tether.

Before he'd even finished speaking a shot was fired, but

the report was so muffled that no one could tell whether it had come from the left, the right, the grounds, the house, the woods or the road.

Then they heard footsteps on the stairs. Carl Andersen was coming down them, stiffly, a hand clamped to his chest, and he was yelling like a madman, 'It's her!'

He was panting . . . His glass eye never moved. No one could tell at whom he was staring so wildly with the other one.

9. The Lineup

For a few seconds, about as long as it took the last echoes of the shot to die away, nothing happened. They were all waiting for another. Carl Andersen walked outside and over to a gravel path.

It was one of the policemen stationed in the grounds who dashed towards the kitchen garden, in the middle of which stood a raised well topped by a pulley. He leaned over it, but quickly jerked back and blew his whistle.

'Take him away, by force if you have to!' Maigret shouted to Lucas, pointing to the tottering Andersen.

In the thin light of dawn, now everything happened at once.

Lucas signalled to one of his men. The two of them approached the wounded man, spoke with him briefly and, as he would not cooperate, tipped him over and carried him away, struggling and protesting hoarsely.

Meanwhile, Maigret was approaching the well but stopped in his tracks when the policeman yelled, 'Watch out!'

And another bullet whistled through the air as the underground report reverberated in long echoing waves.

'Who's down there?'

'The girl . . . and a man. They're fighting hand to hand . . .'

The inspector went over cautiously, but could see almost nothing down the well.

'Your flashlight . . .'

He had time to get only the bricfest impression of what was happening before a bullet almost hit the flashlight.

The man was Michonnet. The well was not deep. It was wide, however, and completely dry.

There were two of them down there, locked in a struggle. As far as Maigret could tell, the insurance agent had a hand around Else's throat as if to strangle her. She had a revolver in one fist, but Michonnet's other hand was around hers, controlling where the gun was aimed.

'What are we going to do?' asked the appalled policeman.

They could hear occasional groans; it was Else, suffocating, battling ferociously.

'Michonnet, give yourself up!' Maigret called out clearly, as a matter of form.

Without a word the other man fired the revolver into the air, and the inspector did not hesitate any longer. The well was three metres deep. Maigret suddenly jumped in, landing literally on Michonnet's back and pinning down one of Else's legs as well.

It was total chaos. One more shot went off, grazing the wall of the well before vanishing into the blue, while Maigret punched Michonnet's skull with both fists, just to be on the safe side. At the fourth blow, the man looked at him like a wounded animal, staggered and fell backwards with a black eye and dislocated jaw.

Else, who was holding her throat with both hands, was gasping for breath.

It was both tragic and absurd, this battle in the murky light at the bottom of a well smelling of saltpetre and slime.

The epilogue was even more absurd: Michonnet was hauled up by the pulley rope, limp and groaning; Else, whom Maigret held up to the policeman, was filthy, her black velvet dress blotched with big smears of greenish moss.

Neither she nor her adversary had completely lost consciousness. They were exhausted and sore, however, like clowns after a fake boxing match who lie collapsed in a disheartened heap together, still swinging feebly at nothing.

Maigret had picked up the revolver. It was Else's, the one taken from the niche in her bedroom. There was one bullet left.

Arriving from the house, Lucas looked worried and sighed as he took in the scene.

'I had to tie him to his bed.'

The policeman had moistened a handkerchief with water and was dabbing the girl's forehead.

'And where'd these two come from?' the sergeant continued.

Suddenly Michonnet, despite not having even enough strength left to stand up, threw himself at Else, his face convulsed with fury. He never reached her, for Maigret gave him a kick that sent him tumbling a good two metres away.

'That's enough of this farce!' he bellowed.

Then he laughed almost to tears, the look on Michonnet's face was so funny. He was like one of those infuriated kids you carry off under your arm, spanking them as you go, yet they keep wriggling, howling, crying, lashing out and trying to bite, refusing to accept that they're helpless.

For Michonnet was crying! Crying and grimacing miserably! He was even shaking his fist!

Else was finally back on her feet, rubbing her hand over her forehead.

'I really thought I was done for,' she sighed, smiling weakly. 'He was squeezing so hard . . .'

One cheek was black with dirt and there was mud in her tangled hair. Maigret wasn't much more presentable.

'What were you doing in the well?' he asked.

She looked at him sharply. Her smile vanished. In a single moment, she seemed to have recovered all her sang-froid.

'Answer me.'

'I . . . I was taken there by force . . .'

'By Michonnet?'

'That's not true!' screamed the man.

'It is true. He tried to strangle me . . . I think he's insane.'

'She's lying! She's the one who's insane! Or rather, she's . . .'

'She's what?'

'I don't know! She's . . . She's a viper whose head should be crushed on a stone!'

Meanwhile, dawn had broken. Birds were twittering in all the trees.

'Why did you take your revolver?' Maigret asked Else.

'Because I was afraid of a trap . . .'

'What trap? Hold on a minute! One thing at a time. You just said that you were attacked and put into the well.'

'She's lying!' repeated Michonnet, gulping convulsively.

'Then show me,' Maigret went on, 'where this attack took place.'

Looking around her, Else pointed over to the front steps.

'It was there? And you didn't scream?'

'I couldn't . . .'

'And this scrawny little fellow managed to carry you all the way over to the well, lugging fifty-five kilos?'

'Yes, it's true.'

'She's lying!'

'Make him be quiet!' she said wearily. 'Don't you see he's crazy? And has been for a while, too.'

They had to restrain Michonnet, who was about to go after her again.

They formed a small group in the kitchen garden: Maigret, Lucas, two inspectors, all looking at the insurance agent with the swollen face and Else, who even while talking had been trying to clean herself up.

For some strange reason, this entire episode had not risen to the level of tragedy, or even drama. It was more like buffoonery.

The feeble morning light might well have had something to do with it. And perhaps everyone's fatigue, even their hunger.

Things got worse when they saw a simple soul walking

hesitantly down the road, a woman who peered through the bars of the front gate, finally opened it and caught sight of Michonnet.

'Émile!' she exclaimed.

It was Madame Michonnet, more bewildered than distressed, who now pulled a hankie from her pocket and burst out crying.

'It's that woman again!'

She looked like someone's good old mother, battered by events and falling back on the soothing bitterness of tears.

Maigret noticed with amusement how Else's face seemed to come into tight focus as she looked at everyone around her in turn. A pretty face, delicate, gone suddenly sharp-featured and tense.

'What were you planning on doing in the well?' he asked cheerfully, as if he were saying, 'Enough of this! Admit it, there's no point in pretending any more.'

She understood. Gave him an ironic smile.

'I think we're done for,' she conceded. 'Only, I'm hungry, I'm thirsty, I'm cold and I'd really like to clean myself up a bit. And then we'll see . . .'

She wasn't playing a part. On the contrary, she was admirably to the point.

All alone in the middle of the group, she was relaxed, watching the pitiful Michonnet and his weeping wife with an amused air, and when she turned to Maigret her eyes said, 'Poor things! Us, we're two of a kind, aren't we! We'll talk later. You've won . . . but admit it: I put on quite a show!'

No fear, no embarrassment, either. No theatrics at all.

It was the real Else at last – and she was enjoying this moment of truth.

'Come along with me,' said Maigret. 'Lucas, you take care of the other one . . . As for his wife, she can go home or stay here, either way.'

'Come in! You're not disturbing me . . .'

It was the same room, up there, with the black divan, the insistent perfume, the hiding place behind the water-colour. It was the same woman.

'Carl is well guarded, at least?' she asked, jerking her chin towards his room. 'Because he'd be even harder to control than Michonnet! . . . You may smoke your pipe.'

She poured some water into the basin, calmly pulled off her dress as if that were the most natural thing in the world, and stood there in her slip, without any fuss or provocation.

Maigret recalled his first visit to the Three Widows house, when Else had been as enigmatic and distant as a cinema vamp, and he remembered the disturbing, enervating atmosphere with which she could surround herself.

Had she played her part well, the alluring, wilful young thing who talked about her parents' castle, the nannies and governesses, her father's strict principles?

Well, that was yesterday! One gesture was more eloquent than any words: the way she'd stripped off her dress and was now looking at herself in the mirror before washing her face.

The classic tart, earthy, vulgar and sly.

'Admit that you fell for it!'

'Not for long!'

She wiped her face with a corner of the Turkish towel.

'Sure! . . . Just yesterday, when you were here and I flashed you a peck at one breast, your mouth was dry and your forehead sweaty, like the nice fat old fellow you are. That won't work with you now, of course. Even though I haven't lost any of my looks . . .'

She threw out her chest and happily admired her lithe and barely clad figure.

'Between us, what tipped you off? I made a mistake?'

'Several.'

'Such as?'

'Talking a mite too much about the castle and the grounds . . . When you really live in a castle, you usually call it the house, for example.'

She had pulled aside the curtain of a wardrobe and was studying her dresses.

'You'll be taking me to Paris, naturally! And there will be photographers there . . . What do you think of this green dress?'

She held it up to herself to judge the effect.

'No: black is still my best colour . . . Will you give me a light?'

She laughed, for, in spite of everything, Maigret was slightly affected by the subtle eroticism she managed to instil in the atmosphere, especially when she went over for him to light her cigarette.

'Well! Time to get dressed . . . The whole thing's a scream, don't you think?'

Her accent made even common slang sound strangely appealing . . .

'How long have you been Carl Andersen's mistress?'

'I am not his mistress. I am his wife.'

She ran a mascara wand along her eyelashes, freshened the pink in her cheeks.

'Were you married in Denmark?'

'You see, you still don't know a thing! And don't count on me to talk, I'm no snitch . . . Anyway, you won't hold me for long. How soon after I'm arrested do I get booked?'

'Right away.'

'Too bad for you! Because they'll find out that my real name is Bertha Krull and that for just over three years now the Copenhagen police have had a warrant out for my arrest. The Danish government will ask for extradition . . . There! I'm ready. Now, if you'll allow me, I'd like a bite to eat . . . Don't you think it smells musty in here?'

She went over to open the window, then came back to the door. Maigret left the bedroom first. She then slammed the door shut, slid the bolt, and he could hear her running to the window.

Had Maigret been ten kilos lighter, she would probably have got away. The bolt had only just gone home when, without losing a second, he hurled himself full tilt against the door.

And it gave way at once, falling flat with its lock and hinges ripped off.

Else was sitting astride the window-sill. She hesitated . . .

'Too late!' he said.

She turned around, breathing a touch heavily, her fore-head slightly damp.

'I don't know why I bothered to dress myself up!' she remarked sarcastically, pointing out a tear in her dress.

'Will you promise me you won't try again to escape?'

'No!'

'In that case, I warn you that I will shoot at the slightest false move.'

And he kept his revolver in his hand from then on.

'Do you think he'll make it?' she asked as they passed Carl's door. 'He's got two bullets in him, hasn't he?'

He looked at her and although at that moment he would have been hard put to read her mind, he thought he detected in her face and voice a mixture of pity and resentment.

'It's his fault too!' she decided, as if to set her conscience at rest. 'I only hope there's still something to eat in the house . . .'

Maigret followed her into the kitchen, where she searched the cupboards and finally unearthed a tin of rock lobster.

'Won't you open it for me? . . . Don't worry, I promise I won't take advantage and make a run for it.'

There was a strangely companionable feeling between the two of them that Maigret rather enjoyed. There was even something intimate in their relationship, and the faintest undercurrent of possibilities.

She was having fun with this big, placid man who had bested her but whom she knew she was impressing with her dash and daring. As for him, he was savouring this most unusual familiarity perhaps a little too much.

'Here you are . . . Eat quickly.'

'We're leaving already?'

'I've no idea.'

'Just between us . . . Exactly what have you found out?'

'Doesn't matter.'

'Are you carting off Michonnet as well, that idiot? Still, he's the one who scared me the most . . . Back in the well I really thought I'd had it. His eyes were bulging out of his head . . . He was squeezing my throat with everything he had.'

'Were you his mistress?'

She shrugged, the kind of girl for whom such details have almost no importance.

'And Monsieur Oscar?' he added.

'What about him?'

'Another lover?'

'You'll have to find all that out by yourself. Me, I know exactly what's waiting for me. I've got five years to do in Denmark: accessory to armed robbery and resisting arrest. That's when I caught this bullet.'

And she pointed to her right breast.

'As for the rest, this lot here will cope on their own!'

'Where did you meet Isaac Goldberg?'

'I've got nothing to say.'

'You'll have to talk at some point . . .'

'And just how do you think you can make me?'

She was answering while eating some rock lobster without any bread, because there was none left in the kitchen. They could hear a policeman walking up and down in the drawing room while he kept an eye on Michonnet, slumped in an armchair.

Two cars pulled up at the same time outside the front gate, which was opened to allow them to come up the drive and around to the front steps.

In the first car sat an inspector, two gendarmes, Monsieur Oscar and his wife.

The other car was the taxi from Paris, in which an inspector was guarding a third person.

The three prisoners were wearing handcuffs, but they kept up a good front, except for the garage owner's wife, whose eyes were red.

Maigret took Else into the drawing room, where Michonnet tried yet again to rush towards her.

The prisoners were brought inside. Monsieur Oscar behaved almost as casually as an ordinary visitor, but he did wince when he saw Else and Michonnet. The other man, who might have been an Italian, decided to brazen it out.

'Great! A family reunion! Are we having a wedding, or reading a will?'

'Luckily, we brought them in without any trouble,' the officer explained to Maigret. 'On the way through Étampes, we picked up two gendarmes who had been informed of the situation and seen the car go past without being able to stop it. Fifty kilometres from Orléans the fugitives had a flat tyre, halted in the middle of the road and trained their revolvers on us . . . The garage owner was the first one to think better of it – otherwise we'd have had quite a gun battle.

'We started towards them; the Italian did fire at us twice with his Browning, but missed.'

'Well, now,' observed Monsieur Oscar. 'In my house, I served you a drink, so allow me to point out that it's rather parched around here . . .'

Maigret had had the mechanic fetched from the garage and seemed to be counting heads.

'All of you go and line up against the wall!' he ordered. 'At the other end, Michonnet . . . No use trying to get near Else.'

The little man glared at him and went to stand at the end of the line, with his drooping moustache and his eye still swelling from all those punches.

Next came the mechanic, whose wrists were still bound by the electric wire. Then the garage owner's wife, thin and woebegone, and the garage owner himself, who was much annoyed at being unable to put his hands into the pockets of his baggy trousers. Finally, Else and the Italian, who must have been the ladies' man of the gang and had a naked woman tattooed on the back of one hand.

Maigret looked them over slowly, one by one, with a satisfied little smile, then filled his spare pipe, strode over to the front steps to open the French windows and called out, 'Take their surnames, given names, occupations and addresses, Lucas . . . Let me know when you're done.'

The six of them stood all lined up. Pointing to Else, Lucas asked, 'Should I cuff her as well?'

'Why not?'

At which Else responded hotly, 'That's really rotten of you, inspector!'

The grounds were brimming with sunshine. Thousands of birds were singing. On the horizon, the weathercock of a little village church steeple was glistening as if it were solid gold.

10. *Looking for a Head*

When Maigret returned to the drawing room, where the wide-open French windows were welcoming the spring air, Lucas was wrapping up his interrogation in an atmosphere not unlike that of a barrack room.

The prisoners were still lined up against a wall, albeit in a less orderly fashion. And at least three of them were acting distinctly unimpressed by their police captors: the garage owner, his mechanic Jojo and the Italian Guido Ferrari.

Monsieur Oscar was dictating to Lucas.

'Occupation: garage proprietor and mechanic. Add on former professional boxer, licensed in 1920. Middleweight champion of Paris in 1922 . . .'

Some officers brought in two new recruits: garage employees who'd just shown up as usual for work. They were placed in the lineup with the others. One of them, who had the mug of a gorilla, simply drawled, 'That's it? We're busted?'

They were all talking at once, like children when their teacher is out of the room. They nudged one another with their elbows and cracked jokes.

Only Michonnet still presented a sorry sight, hunched over and glowering at the floor.

As for Else, she watched Maigret almost as if he were

her accomplice. Hadn't they understood each other remarkably well? Whenever Monsieur Oscar made a bad pun, she smiled discreetly at the inspector.

As far as she was concerned, she was a cut above all this.

'Let's have some silence, now!' thundered Maigret.

But at that same moment, a small sedan drew up at the front steps. The driver was well dressed and carried a leather instrument case under his arm with an air of importance. He came briskly up the steps only to stare in astonishment at the row of suspects that suddenly confronted him.

'The patient?'

'Would you take care of this, Lucas?'

It was an eminent surgeon from Paris, called in to attend to Carl Andersen. He went off with a worried look while the sergeant led the way.

'D'ja catch the look on that doc's kisser?'

Only Else had frowned, and her eyes had gone a little less blue . . .

'I called for silence!' said Maigret clearly. 'Save the wise-cracks for later. What you seem to be forgetting is that at least one of you looks likely to pay for this with his head.'

And he looked slowly up and down the line. His speech had produced the desired effect.

The sun was the same; there was spring in the air. The birds kept on chirping in the trees and the shade from the foliage still trembled on the gravel path.

In the drawing room, though, one felt that mouths had gone drier, that cheekiness was draining away . . .

Still, Michonnet was the only one who moaned, and so

unwittingly that he was himself the most surprised of all and turned his head aside, embarrassed.

'I can see you've understood!' continued Maigret, beginning to pace the room with his hands behind his back. 'We'll try to save time. If we're unsuccessful here, we'll keep going at Quai des Orfèvres . . . You must know the place, right? Good! . . . First crime: Isaac Goldberg is shot at point-blank range. Who brought Goldberg to the Three Widows Crossroads?'

They were silent, all looking at one another with no love lost, while over their heads the surgeon could be heard moving around.

'I'm waiting! I repeat: we'll continue this at police headquarters – and there, you'll be grilled one by one . . . Goldberg was in Antwerp. There was about two million in diamonds to unload . . . Who got the ball rolling?'

'I did!' said Else. 'I'd met Goldberg in Copenhagen. I knew stolen jewels were his specialty. When I read about the burglary in London and the papers said the diamonds had to be in Antwerp, I assumed Goldberg was in on it. I talked to Oscar about it . . .'

'Thanks a lot!' muttered the garage owner.

'Who wrote the letter to Goldberg?'

'She did.'

'Let's keep going . . . He arrives during the night. Who's at the garage at that point? . . . And most importantly, whose job is it to kill him?'

Silence. The sound of Lucas coming downstairs to speak to an officer.

'Hop it to Arpajon,' he told the officer, 'and bring back

the first doctor you can find to help the professor, along with some camphorated oil. Got that?'

Lucas headed back upstairs while Maigret, his brow furrowed, studied his flock.

'We'll jump back a little in time . . . I think that will be simpler. You: when did you become a fence?'

He was looking hard at the garage owner, who seemed to find this question less prickly than the previous ones.

'That's it! Now you're talking! You admit yourself that I'm nothing but a fence. And maybe not even that . . .'

He was an incredible ham. He looked from one to another of the others, trying to make them smile.

'My wife and I, we're practically honest folks. Right, honey? . . . It's quite simple: I was a boxer. I lost my title in 1925 – and all I got offered was a job at the Foire du Thrône fairgrounds in Paris! Not nearly enough for me. We had some friends who were legit and some who weren't. One guy – he was arrested two years later – was raking it in at the time, selling stuff he'd got on credit.

'I thought I'd try that, but since I'd been a mechanic when I was younger, I decided to start with garages, thinking I'd get my hands on cars, tyres, spare parts, sell it all on the quiet and clear off. I was counting on making 400,000 or so!

'Trouble was, I was late out of the gate. The big places were thinking twice before letting the goods leave home on credit.

'I got brought a stolen car to freshen up . . . A guy I'd met in a bar near the Bastille. You can't imagine how easy it is!

'Word got around in Paris. I was in a cushy spot, seeing as I'd hardly any neighbours. I turned ten or twenty cars around . . . Then one turned up, I can still see it today: full of silverware stolen from a villa around Bougival. We squirrelled that lot away, got in touch with second-hand dealers in Étampes, Orléans and even farther away.

'We got used to this routine . . . A sweet racket . . .'

'Has he found out about the tyres yet?' he asked, turning towards Jojo, who sighed.

'He sure has . . .'

'You know how wacky you look with your electric wire? Add a plug and you'd be a blinking lamp!'

Maigret cut him off.

'Isaac Goldberg arrived in his own car, a Minerva. There was a welcoming party, because the idea wasn't to buy his diamonds, even on the cheap, but to steal them. And to do that you had to bump him off. So there was a bunch of you in the garage, that's to say in the house behind it . . .'

Absolute silence. This was the sore spot. Once again Maigret looked them all in the face one by one . . . and saw a few drops of sweat on the Italian's forehead.

'You're the killer, right?'

'No! It's . . . It's . . .'

'Who?'

'It's them, it's . . .'

'He's lying!' yelled Monsieur Oscar.

'Who got the nod?'

Shrugging cockily, the garage owner said, 'The guy upstairs, so there!'

'Say that again!'

'The guy upstairs!'

But he didn't sound as sure of himself this time around.

'Else, come over here!'

Maigret pointed to Else, with the confidence of a conductor with the most diverse instruments at his command who knows his motley orchestra will still perform in perfect harmony.

'You were born in Copenhagen?'

'If you keep using my name, chief inspector, everyone will think we slept together . . .'

'Answer me.'

'Hamburg!'

'What was your father's occupation?'

'Docker.'

'He's still alive?'

Her whole body shuddered. She looked at her companions with a sort of uneasy pride.

'They cut his head off, in Düsseldorf.'

'Your mother?'

'A drunk.'

'What were you doing in Copenhagen?'

'I was a sailor's girl. Hans! A handsome fellow I'd met in Hamburg. He took me along with him. He belonged to a gang. One day we decided to knock over a bank, had it all set up. We were supposed to get millions in a single night. I was the lookout . . . But someone snitched on us, because just when the men started in on the safes, the cops surrounded us.

'It was at night, you couldn't see a thing . . . We were scattered . . . There were shots; people yelling, chasing us.

I got hit in the chest and began to run. Two policemen grabbed me. I bit one of them, kicked the other in the stomach and he let me go . . .

'But I was still being chased. And then I saw a wall: I hauled myself up . . . I literally fell off the other side and when I came to there was a tall young man, very chic, upper-class, looking at me with bewilderment and pity . . .'

'Andersen?'

'That isn't his real name. He'll tell you *that* only if it suits him to. It's a well-known name . . . They're people with entrée to the royal court, who spend half the year in one of the most lovely castles in Denmark and the other half in a great mansion with grounds as large as an entire city neighbourhood.'

An officer arrived accompanied by a short, flushed, pop-eyed man. It was the doctor requested by the surgeon. He stopped short before the strange gathering, especially at the sight of handcuffs on almost everyone's hands, but he was hustled on up to the first floor.

'After that . . .'

Monsieur Oscar snickered. Else gave him a fierce, almost venomous look.

'They can't understand,' she murmured. 'Carl hid me in his parents' mansion and took care of me himself, with a friend who was studying medicine. He had already lost an eye in that plane crash. He wore a black monocle . . . I think he considered himself permanently disfigured. He was convinced that no woman could love him, that whenever he had to remove his black eyeglass, revealing his sewn-up eyelid and fake eye, he would become repulsive . . .'

'Did he love you?'

'It wasn't exactly that. I didn't understand at first . . . and they,' she added, pointing to her accomplices, 'will never understand. It was a Protestant family. Carl's first impulse was to save a soul, as he put it . . . He made long speeches, read me chapters from the Bible. Yet at the same time, Carl was afraid of his parents. Then one day, when I was almost well again, he suddenly kissed me on the mouth – and ran away. I didn't see him for almost a week. Well, I was able to watch him from the dormer window of a servant's room where I was kept hidden . . . He walked for hours in the garden with his head hanging, visibly unhappy.'

Monsieur Oscar was actually slapping his thighs in delight.

'It's just like a novel!' he exclaimed. 'Keep going, honeybunch!'

'That's all there is . . . When he came to see me again he said he wanted to marry me, that he couldn't do that in his country, that we were going abroad . . . He claimed that he had understood at last what life was all about, that he had found his reason for living and would no longer be a useless human being . . . And stuff like that . . .'

Her voice was becoming more common again.

'We got married in Holland under the name of Andersen. I was enjoying myself. I think I even fell for his fairy tale, too. He would tell me the most amazing things . . . He made me dress like this, like that, learn table manners, ditch my accent . . . He had me read books. We used to visit museums.'

'How about that, my angel!' Monsieur Oscar exclaimed to his wife. 'When we're sprung from the big house, we'll go and visit museums too, won't we? And hold hands, making sheep's eyes at the Mona Lisa . . .'

'We came to live out here,' Else went on quickly, 'because Carl was always afraid of running into one of my old accomplices. He had to work because he'd renounced his parents' fortune. As a precaution, he passed me off as his sister, but he still worried . . . Whenever anyone rang at the front gate it made him jump, because Hans managed to escape from prison and no one knows what happened to him . . . Carl loves me, that's for sure.'

'And yet . . .' said Maigret thoughtfully.

'I'd like to see what you'd have done here!' snapped Else. 'Alone, always alone! With nothing but talk about goodness, beauty, the salvation of the soul, human destiny and being worthy of the Lord . . . And those lessons in deportment! And when he went anywhere he locked me in, supposedly to save me from temptation. The truth is he was ferociously possessive . . . and passionate, too!'

'Now no one can say I don't know a good thing when I see it!' crowed Monsieur Oscar.

'And what did you do?' Maigret asked him.

'I spotted her, for God's sake! It was easy: I could tell she was putting on all those fancy manners. For a while I even wondered if the Danish fellow wasn't a fake as well. But I didn't trust him. I preferred to sniff around the tart . . . Oh, now honey, don't get upset, you know

I've always come back to you in the end! The other stuff is just business. Anyway, I used to prowl around that dump when ol' One-Eye wasn't there. We started talking one day, her at the window, being as the bird was in a cage. She saw right away how matters stood. I tossed her a ball of wax to take an impression of her lock . . . The next month we met at the far end of the grounds to talk shop. No magic needed! She was sick of that blue-blood of hers . . . She had a hankering for her old life is all!'

'And since then,' said Maigret slowly to Else, 'you've been regularly slipping veronal into Carl Andersen's food at night?'

'Yes . . .'

'And you would go to meet Oscar?'

The garage owner's wife had red eyes but was holding back her tears.

'They deceived me, chief inspector! At first my husband told me she was just a pal, that rescuing her from that hole was really a good deed! Then he used to take us both for evenings out in Paris, we'd have wild times with our friends . . . I never suspected a thing until the day I . . . found them . . .'

'And so what? All men aren't monks . . . She was wasting away, poor dear.'

Else was quiet. There was a sad look in her eyes, and she seemed uneasy.

Suddenly Lucas came back downstairs.

'Are there any methylated spirits in the house?'

'What for?'

'To disinfect the instruments.'

It was Else who rushed to the kitchen and looked through all the bottles.

'I found it! . . . Are they going to save him? Is he in any pain?'

'Filthy bitch!' growled Michonnet, who had been dead to the world since the beginning of this interrogation.

Looking Michonnet straight in the eye, Maigret asked the garage owner, 'And this one?'

'You haven't figured that out yet?'

'Just about . . . There are three houses at the crossroads. Every night was suspiciously full of comings and goings: the vegetable lorries, coming back unloaded from Paris, were bringing in the stolen goods. The Three Widows house posed no threat, but the villa . . .'

'Not to mention that we needed someone respectable to sell certain items out in the countryside.'

'So Else was assigned to rope in Michonnet?'

'Why waste a pretty girl? He was swept off his feet! She brought him along one night and we reeled him in with champagne. Another time we took him to Paris for one of our best blow-outs, while his wife thought he was off on a tour of inspection. He was done for! Take it or leave it, we told him. The best part was that he thought she'd fallen for him and he turned as jealous as a schoolboy. Isn't that the limit? And him with the mug of a department store cashier!'

There was some kind of noise upstairs and Maigret saw Else go dead white. From then on she ignored the interrogation and listened intently to the proceedings overhead.

They heard the surgeon's voice.

'Hold him . . .'

Outside, two sparrows were hopping around on the white gravel path.

Filling a pipe, Maigret reviewed the prisoners once again.

'Now all we need to know is, who the killer was . . . Quiet!'

'In my case, for fencing, I shouldn't get more than—'

The inspector silenced Monsieur Oscar with an impatient glare.

'Else learns from the papers that the jewellery stolen in London and valued at two million must be in the possession of Isaac Goldberg, whom she met when she belonged to the gang in Copenhagen. She writes to him to set up a meeting at the garage, with a promise to purchase the diamonds at a good price . . . Goldberg, who remembers her from before, does not suspect trouble and arrives in his car.

'Champagne is served, in the house . . . Reinforcements have been called in – in other words, you are all there. The problem is getting rid of the corpse, once the murder has been committed . . .

'Michonnet must be nervous, because, for the first time, he'll be involved in a real crime . . . But he is probably given more champagne than the others.

'Oscar's probably for dumping the body in a ditch someplace far away.

'It's Else who comes up with an idea . . . Quiet! . . . She's had enough of living locked in during the day and having to hide at night. She's had enough of the speeches about virtue, goodness and beauty! She's also had enough of her boring life, and of counting each sou . . .

'She's come to hate Carl Andersen. But she knows he loves her enough to kill her rather than lose her.

'She's drinking! She's flying high! She has a bold, exciting idea: to pin the crime on Carl! On Carl, who is so blinded by love that he will never even suspect her.

'Isn't that so, Else?'

For the first time, she turned her head away.

'The Minerva, disguised by Oscar's crew, will be sent far away to be sold or abandoned. The real culprits must be placed beyond suspicion. And Michonnet is the most afraid! His car will therefore be "stolen", which is the best way to camouflage him. He'll be the one to complain first to the police, fretting about the disappearance of his six-cylinder car. But the police must also go looking for the corpse over at Carl's place. And that's when someone has the bright idea of switching the cars.

'The corpse is installed at the wheel of Michonnet's car. Andersen, as usual, has been drugged and is fast asleep. The car is driven into his garage. The little jalopy is placed inside Michonnet's.

'The police will be flummoxed! And even better, this aloof Danish fellow passes among the locals for half mad . . . The country folk are spooked by his black monocle.

'Suspicion will fall on him! And everything about this case is so bizarre that it will fit his appearance and reputation like a glove. Besides, after his arrest, won't he kill himself to avoid the scandal that might reflect upon his family if his true identity were ever discovered?'

The little doctor from Arpajon poked his head around the half-open door.

'Another man, to hold him . . . We're having trouble putting him to sleep . . .'

The doctor was flushed, impatient. There was an officer out in the garden.

'You go!' Maigret shouted to him.

And at that same moment received an unexpected blow to the chest.

11. *Else*

It was Else, who had flung herself on him, sobbing convulsively, pleading with him.

'I don't want him to die!' she stammered. 'Please! . . . I . . . This is awful . . .'

The moment was so gripping and she seemed so truly sincere that the others, those sinister men lined up against the wall, neither sneered nor even smiled.

'Let me go upstairs! I'm begging you! You can't understand . . .'

But Maigret pushed her aside! She went to collapse on the dark divan where he'd seen her that first time, an enigmatic figure in her high-necked black velvet dress.

'I'm nearly done! . . . Michonnet played his part perfectly. And all the more believably in that he had to act like a ridiculous little fellow caught up in a bloody crime who thinks only of his car. The police investigation begins; Carl Andersen is arrested. And it just so happens that he does not commit suicide and is even released.

'Not for a moment has he suspected his wife. He will never suspect her. He would defend her even against all evidence.

'But now we learn that Madame Goldberg, who might know and reveal who drew her husband into this trap, is coming here.

'The same man who shot the diamond merchant lies in wait for her . . .'

The chief inspector looked at his audience one by one, then pressed on as if in a hurry to be done with it.

'The murderer has put on Carl's shoes, which will be found here covered in mud from the field . . . That's overdoing things! But Carl must be found guilty or else the real murderers will soon be unmasked. Now panic sets in.

'Andersen has to go to Paris because he needs money. The same man who committed the first two crimes waits for him along his route and, posing as a policeman, gets into his car beside him.

'It isn't Else who came up with that . . . I have the feeling it's Oscar.

'Does he talk to Andersen about escorting him to the border, or confronting him with some witness in a town up north?

'Andersen is made to drive across Paris. The Compiègne road goes through dense woods. The murderer shoots, again at point-blank range. No doubt he hears another car behind them . . . and in a rush he pushes the body out into the roadside ditch. On the way back he'll conceal the body more carefully.

'The immediate concern is to divert all suspicion. That's been done. Andersen's car is abandoned a few hundred metres from the Belgian border.

'The police naturally conclude that – he fled the country! So he is guilty . . .

'The murderer returns with another car. The victim is

no longer in the ditch and there are tracks suggesting that he isn't dead.

'The man assigned to this murder telephones Monsieur Oscar from Paris: he refuses to come anywhere near this area again, it's too full of cops.

'Carl's devotion to his wife is now common knowledge. If he's alive, he'll come back. If he comes back, he might talk . . .

'They have to finish the job. No one feels up to it. Monsieur Oscar doesn't like to get his hands dirty . . .

'Isn't this the moment to use up Michonnet? The man who has sacrificed everything to his love for Else and can be set up to take the last fall?

'The plan is carefully crafted. Monsieur Oscar and his wife go off to Paris, very publicly, describing their intentions in detail.

'Monsieur Michonnet sends for me and shows that he is immobilized in his armchair by gout.

'He has probably read some crime novels. He uses tricks now, just as he does in his insurance dealings. I've hardly left the house when a broomstick and ball of rags have replaced him in the chair – and this stage setting works. From outside, the illusion is flawless . . . And Madame Michonnet, terrorized, agrees to play along by pretending, behind the shade, to take care of the invalid.

'She knows there is a woman involved, and she is jealous, too. But she wants to save her husband in spite of everything because she still hopes he'll come back to her.

'She's not mistaken: Michonnet has sensed that he's

been played for a fool. He no longer knows if he loves or hates Else, but he does know that he wants her dead.

'He knows the house, the grounds, all the ways in or out . . . Perhaps he knows that Else usually drinks some beer in the evening.

'He leaves a poisoned bottle open in the kitchen. He lies in wait outdoors for Carl's return.

'He fires at him . . . He is near collapse. There are policemen everywhere. He winds up hiding in the well, which dried up long ago.

'All that was only a few hours ago. And meanwhile, Madame Michonnet has had to play her part, follow certain instructions . . . If something fishy happens around the garage, she must telephone the Chope Saint-Martin in Paris.

'Well, I turn up. She sees me go inside the garage. I fire off some shots . . . and she turns off the light, warning the drivers in the gang not to stop.

'The telephone call works. Monsieur Oscar, his wife and Guido, who goes along with them, jump into a car with their revolvers and drive by here at top speed, trying to shoot me dead since I might well be the only person who knows something.

'They take the road to Étampes and Orléans. Why? When they could flee via another route, in a different direction?

'Because along that road travels a lorry carrying a spare tyre collected from the mechanic . . . *and that tyre contains the diamonds!*

'They must catch up with the lorry and only then, their pockets full, make for the border . . .

'So far so good? . . . Be quiet: I'm not asking *you* anything! . . . Michonnet is down his well. Else, who knows the grounds, suspects that he's hiding there. She knows he's the one who tried to poison her. She harbours no illusions about the fellow. Arrested, he will spill everything. So she decides to get rid of him.

'Did she accidentally fall in? In any case, she ends up in the well with him, holding a revolver. But he grabs her throat with one hand . . . and gets the other around the wrist of her gun hand. They struggle in the darkness. A shot is fired . . . Else cries out in spite of herself, because she's afraid of dying.'

He struck a safety match to relight his pipe.

'What do you say to that, Monsieur Oscar?'

'I'll defend myself,' he said glumly. 'I'm not saying anything . . . except that I'm just a fence.'

'He's lying!' yelped his neighbour, Guido Ferrari.

'Ah! . . . You, I was waiting for you, pal. Because you're the shooter! All three times! First you shot Goldberg, then his wife, and finally, in the car, Carl Andersen. Oh, yes! You're a hired gun if ever I saw one.'

'Not true!'

'Calm down . . .'

'It's not true! Not true! . . . I don't want . . .'

'You're fighting for your life, but Carl Andersen will soon identify you . . . and the others will abandon you. They're not looking at anything but jail time.'

Then Guido drew himself up, pointed at the garage owner and exclaimed viciously, 'He's the one who gave the orders!'

'Goddamn you!'

And before Maigret could step in, Monsieur Oscar had slammed his handcuffed fists down on the Italian's skull, yelling, 'You scum! You'll pay for that . . .'

They must have lost their balance because they wound up on the floor, still thrashing around grimly, but the handcuffs made them clumsy.

That was the moment the surgeon chose to come downstairs.

He was wearing a light-grey hat and gloves to match.

'I beg your pardon . . . I was told that the chief inspector was here.'

'That's me.'

'It's about the wounded man . . . I believe he'll pull through. But he must have absolute quiet. I suggested my clinic, but it would seem that it's not possible. In half an hour at the most he will be coming to, and I would recommend—'

A shriek. The Italian was biting the nose of the garage owner, whose wife rushed to Maigret.

'Quick! See what . . .'

The two men were kicked apart while the surgeon, aloof, lips pursed in disgust, walked out to his car and started the engine.

Michonnet was crying quietly in his corner, refusing to look around him.

Grandjean arrived.

'The police van's here.'

The culprits were bundled outside, one after the other. Gone were the sneers and any effort at bravado. At the back of the van there was almost a fresh scuffle between the Italian and the man next to him, a mechanic from the garage.

'Thieves! Thugs!' shouted the Italian, crazed with fear. 'I never even got the money you promised me!'

Else was the last to go. At the moment when, reluctantly, she was about to step through the French windows on to the sunlit steps, Maigret stopped her with a single word.

'Well?'

She turned towards him, then looked up at the ceiling. Towards the room where Carl was lying.

It was impossible to say whether she would start crying again or muttering curses.

A rather long silence. Maigret was looking her in the eye.

'In the end . . . No! I don't want to say anything bad about him.'

'Say it!'

'You know . . . It's his own fault! He's half mad. He was intrigued when he learned that my father was a thief, that I was part of a gang. That's the only reason he loved me . . . And if I'd become the well-behaved young woman he tried to make of me, he would quickly have lost interest and ditched me . . .'

She turned her face away to add in a soft voice, almost bashfully, 'Still, I wouldn't like anything bad to happen to him . . . He's . . . How can I put it . . . He's a nice guy . . . And slightly cracked!'

And she smiled.

'I suppose I'll be seeing you . . .'

'It was Guido who did the killing, right?'

He'd gone too far. Her expression hardened again.

'I'm no squealer.'

Maigret followed her with his eyes until she climbed into the police van. He saw her look back at the Three Widows house, shrug and toss a joke at the gendarme hustling her along.

'We could call this the case of the three mistakes!' he told Lucas, who was standing at his side.

'Whose mistakes?'

'Else's, first of all, when she straightened the snowy landscape, smoked downstairs, brought the phonograph up to her bedroom, *where she was supposedly locked in* – and when she felt she was in danger, she accused Carl while pretending to defend him.

'The insurance agent's mistake, when he sent for me to show that he would be spending the night at his window.

'Jojo the mechanic's mistake, when he saw me suddenly turn up and, fearing I might discover everything, sent a driver away with a spare wheel full of diamonds that was *too small for the lorry*.

'Otherwise . . .'

'Otherwise? . . .'

'Well, when a woman like Else lies with such perfection that she winds up believing her own story . . .'

'I told you so!'

'Yes . . . She could have become something extraordinary. If that fire inside her hadn't flared back up at times, as though that criminal underworld were calling to her . . .'

Carl Andersen hung for almost a month between life and death. Learning of his condition, his family seized their chance to bring him back to Denmark, where they placed him in a convalescent home that bore a strong resemblance to a lunatic asylum. He did not, therefore, appear in Paris as a witness at the trial.

To everyone's surprise, the request for Else's extradition was refused; she had first to spend three years in the women's prison of Saint-Lazare in Paris.

It was in the visiting room there that Maigret found Andersen arguing with the prison warden three months later, presenting his marriage licence and demanding permission to see the prisoner.

He had hardly changed at all. He still wore his black monocle, but his right shoulder was now a little stiffer.

Catching sight of the inspector, he became flustered and turned his face away.

'Your parents let you leave again?'

'My mother died. I received an inheritance.'

It was his, that limousine parked fifty metres from the prison, with a chauffeur in a fancy uniform behind the wheel.

'And you're still trying, in spite of everything?'

'I'm moving to Paris.'

'To come and visit her?'

'She is my wife . . .'

And his single eye searched Maigret's face in dread of finding irony or pity there . . .

The inspector simply shook his hand.

At the prison in Melun, two women would arrive together for their visits like inseparable friends.

'He's not a bad fellow,' Oscar's wife would say. 'He's even too kind, too generous. He gives twenty-franc tips to café waiters! That's what did him in. That and women!'

'Before he met that woman, Monsieur Michonnet would never have filched a single sou from a client. But he swore to me last week that he never even thinks of her now . . .'

On Death Row, Guido Ferrari spent his time waiting for his lawyer to arrive, bearing his pardon. But one morning, five men appeared instead to carry him away, struggling and screaming.

He refused the cigarette and the glass of rum, then spat at the chaplain.

OTHER TITLES IN THIS SERIES

And more to follow

www.penguin.com